HAN M GREENBARG

Riverduna

First published by starlighteineadhpress 2022

This novel is entirely a work of fiction. The names, characters and incidents portrayed in it are the work of the author's imagination. Any resemblance to actual persons, living or dead, events or localities is entirely coincidental.

First edition

ISBN: 979-8-98-660444-2

This book was professionally typeset on Reedsy.
Find out more at reedsy.com

For the survivors. You are warriors in more ways than you know. Trust the high ground. Always believe in your heart that deliverance will come. Deliverance will come for all.

Contents

Note On Pronunciation

The word Paedor may, in fact, be pronounced as 'Pee-ter' in some cases, but for the purpose of this story, the correct pronunciation is 'Pay-dor'.

I

Part One: The Raven

1

Riverduna

I blindly run, scrambling across the rooftops, hoping to catch up with my new friend. The night fog veils every silhouette. "Come back! I didn't get your name!"

The gaps between the rooftops are my favorite. That's when I get to vault like an excited fawn and land in a chaotic tumble on the other side. The running jump is the best I think, but my big brothers always preferred to shove each other off the edge and see who was most graceful in their descent.

"Where'd you go?"

Chasing the critters up here… squirrels, raccoons, sparrows. And dancing with fireflies. I've done this ever since I could walk. I can't lie and say it doesn't get boring or lonely. It does. But I'm their friend and they're mine.

"Darn it." I slide to the edge, perching cautiously like a hawk in her nest. Nothing moves beneath me. No voices rise up, animal or otherwise. I stand and blink hard in the sudden rush of wind. It's safer in the attic. But I hate being inside any building for longer than a day.

"Fireflies." I follow the tiny lights in the opposite direction, keeping my feet aligned with the edge. "C'mon, go this way!"

It's eight months into my seventeenth year and I still repeat the nightly routine from childhood. Peaceful except for the echoing noises from below. The noise of Dredgar. I've never seen a fight. Only heard them. But they always sound like tortured beasts in a cage. Insane and uncivilized, as Mama described them.

But sometimes I long for company. Even if it was among the uncivilized. I don't really think they are all murderous fighters or that they're thirsty for blood as Father had told me. How could hundreds of people down there, the Paedors, all have a cruel heart? I would love to speak with a Paedor instead of continuing all my one-sided conversations with rats and squirrels. I'm tired of falling asleep in the cold and waking up alone.

"All right," I say to the sky. I can't stop shivering. "You win again. I'll sleep inside tonight."

We pride ourselves on moving like shadows, and once inside a house, we Skies try not to make a sound beyond munching food or snoring. Paedors aren't supposed to know that we use their attics for rest. Some might notice traces of our belongings, but I make a point to leave only one thing at a time in each attic. I've memorized every inch of rooftop up here in Nameus, and within fourteen of the attics I've placed special plush toys as a sign to other Skies that it's a safe place to fall asleep.

"'Abby's sixth birthday,'" I read aloud from my makeshift bed on the damp, creaky floor. Another blurry photograph with the year 1989 scrawled next to the other two lines of writing. The image is of a little brown-haired girl in overalls and hair bows and she's looking at a pink cake with six bright candles. The space around her is dark, but her smile is clear in the photograph. "'We love you, angel girl,'" I whisper the other words on the back. Her parents must've written this. I wonder what they looked like. How their voices sounded.

"Angel girl," I say to myself as I try to fall asleep. There's not much to look at on the ceiling, save for a few cobwebs, so I keep looking at the photograph until my arms are too tired to hold it up. Every photograph I find I either keep in my trouser pockets or store in the cracks of walls. Some of them get ruined from the rain, but I like having people close by. I like reading the notes and thinking about the decades of life that existed before my world. They had families. Friends. They didn't have to walk for days to forage food. I have a photograph of a vehicle from the year 2007. It's blurry the same as other photographs but it's a pretty color metal. Four wheels. I don't know who it belonged to but I like it.

The Paedors don't seem to store much in their attics, but sometimes I find large cracks in the walls that hide old books and children's plushie toys. I usually fall asleep on the splintery floor hugging a toy bear or dog to my chest. I've seen children in photographs holding their toys this way, and now I understand why.

Mama and Father would find me a new toy on each birthday until I lost them… I sleep the best to the sounds of thunder, rain, and the fuzzy warmth of a toy animal. It makes me happy knowing that all the other Skies are doing the same thing tonight in attics spread across a hundred miles in Nameus. I'm not alone in spirit. *I'm safe. I should be happy every night that I'm safe.*

2

Dunn

Fighting is instinct. Instinct and a mental game.

"Charge him, Dunn!"

"Bite his legs!"

When I'm the middle of a brawl I don't think about much. I take each hit without flinching, and I deliver my own without mercy. No one is kind in Dredgar. Not even my best friend Current.

"C'mon, brother! Get up!"

He's the reason I have one eye…and he never lets me forget which of us is the bigger opponent. I'm five feet four inches. He's six and a half with a build made for choking people out and kicking in heads. But I have my own secret weapon. Sharp teeth. Half of them metal.

"Call it! Call it! Let him have the win!"

Some Paedors joke that I'm a vampire because of my teeth but I swear I'm not. The unnatural parts of me were built in like finer pieces of a clock. Everything works the way it should until someone knocks it out, and when I have to replace an incisor, I do it with the help of a medically talented Ravabrig named Wheelden. Pain like fire, healing like hell, but it gets fixed. And then I give him a swift kick in the groin from the chair for exacerbating my agony.

"Another fight lived, Dunn," Vilho says as I exit the pit. He offers his hand when he sees me slip on the ladder.

"I'm good," I say.

"You're the best entertainment we got, ya know."

I half-smile, nodding as I make my way to the streets. After the fight, win or lose, I have to fulfill my other duty as lamplighter. My short stature doesn't serve me well in lighting lamps, but I do the work to create necessary pools of light along the cobblestone path. I'm always jumped by a ruffian while reaching up with my pole. And I make them regret it every time. Headbutting, brass-knuckling, biting any skin that's in my line of sight.

"Ow! Stupid Dunn!"

I look down at the boy who had just tried to stab my leg with a pocket knife. "Coald, you know better than to attack from behind."

He looks at me while holding his wounded nose. "Why'd you have to kick so hard?"

"Because you never learn your lesson. They sent you to get me again, didn't they?"

"Current says I have to earn my place in the gang."

"That's real gracious of him," I grumble. "Sending a child to do his work. If he wants me to lose another body part, he can just duel me himself."

"Current says you're the best fighter in Dredgar. You always win."

"Usually. Not always."

"He said it's my job to make you stay humble."

"By knifing me in the leg?"

"I chose it."

"And why am I the target?" I ask.

"Current thinks you're not loyal." Coald gives a little growl seeing blood smeared on his hand. He wipes his nose again and winces. "He says you're too soft on people, Dunn."

"You're nine," I say. "You shouldn't have to do this kind of thing."

"They don't care about age."

I step carefully off the ladder, sighing when my boots touch cobblestone. "Okay, bud, just tell them that I conceded to your strike."

He scrunches his face and more blood streams from his nose. "They won't believe that."

"Then I'll give myself a black eye and show Current tomorrow. I'll say that you gave it to me."

"But that's not fair."

I kneel and grip his shoulders, making sure he is looking right into my eye. "You shouldn't have to get beat up because of me."

"I'm not scared of the them. They're nice to me."

They're nice as long as you keep doing their bidding. "Tell them I conceded."

He grins as we do our special handshake. The handshake I made popular with all the children on the streets. "Will do, Dunn."

"Good," I say. "Now go home."

* * *

I start feeling hungry when I'm a few steps from my house. It's been twelve hours since I ate but I don't think about food until I'm well away from the fight pit. The intermingling scents of blood, vomit, and body odor shut down my appetite as long as I'm in survival mode.

"Sorry I'm late," I say as I close the door behind me. I immediately go to Tempest sitting in the rocking chair and take my baby sister from her arms.

"I just got her back to sleep, Dunn. She was fussing for two hours."

"Well, I have her now. You can go."

Tempest stands, taking a moment to fix her frizzy hair and smooth the wrinkles out of her mauve skirt. She walks with a bit of a stagger, struggling to balance herself as she goes to retrieve the shotgun positioned near the front door. I know she drinks a bit too much wine for a nanny, but I have no one else to watch Katlene when I'm out. Tempest has been a good friend to my family and Mama trusted her since before the baby was born.

"Get home safe," I say.

She half-grins and lifts the shotgun over her shoulder. "You know I never walk these streets without Warpetal."

"Yes." I chuckle at her drunken confidence. "The famous shotgun of Tempest Andriksen. How can I forget that?"

She waves at me with her back turned. "I'll see you tomorrow." And when the door slams shut I hear her muffled voice outside. "Sleep a little tonight, won't you, Duncan? Your mind is always turning."

"I'll do my best," I say.

Katlene stays quiet as I rock her in front of the dying fire. It's too late to stir up the embers again, but I'm tempted to do so, feeling her little body shiver in my arms. I pace back and forth, hoping to see her eyes close as I tell her about my day and the winnings I brought home from the fights.

The winnings are always food scraps and rum. I would starve if I wasn't a champion Cruftetin fighter, and by now, the crowds know exactly what they should bring to throw at my feet in the end. It's all for me and my baby sister. I tell myself every morning that I'm doing this for her, and every night when I come home, I promise her that I will always protect her from the darkness of the streets.

"I'll have to hurt myself again to make him happy," I whisper to her in the rocking chair. "Knife cut, bullet wound, something."

Prove my loyalty. Or he'll enslave us both.

3

Riverduna

Sunshine rarely comes to Nameus. The same fog and chill from the night before greet me when I make my trek along the edge. I hold my arms out for balance to keep from slipping on the slate. The birds are making their morning racket across the skyline, their joyful sounds echoing for miles, and I try to spot one as I journey to the southern river. I'm barely a mile into my walk when I see a raven hopping around.

"Good morning, critter," I whisper, crouching down. "Come here."

He hops toward me, head tilting as I talk softly to him.

"Did you fly up from Dredgar?" My fingers are close to touching the tip of wing. "Come on. You can go to the river with me." I reach forward, my hand slapping the air as he screeches and flaps his wings.

"Gotcha, Illdam!" A man suddenly shoots up from the edge, grabbing the raven whilst pulling himself up on the slate.

He's an exceptionally tall man. A Paedor. He surveys his surroundings before whistling sharply and letting the raven go. I watch in silence as it flies back down to Dredgar.

"Well," the tall Paedor says with a wide grin. "Look at this sweet girl."

I step back, startled at the speed in which he follows. I'm a stranger to him but he doesn't seem to think he's a stranger to me. He holds a hand over his chest, speaking to me as if I were a lost child. "My name is Current."

I've never seen a Paedor before. I don't know what to say back or if I should speak at all. But this is what I've wanted. He's appeared out of nowhere.

"Come now, sweetlie," he says. His broad shoulders block the morning light as I gaze up at his face. "Won't you talk to me?"

"Riverduna."

"Is that your name?"

"Yes." I take another step back, reaching the angled part of the rooftops. I pause and take a breath to steady myself.

"Do you know how beautiful you are?"

This man is not giving me space to breathe. He keeps coming closer, pushing me to the opposite edge where I will end up sliding. I don't fear the ground, but I have yet to know his name or whether he is friendly.

"I'm not going to hurt you," he says. "I promise."

A person's word means absolutely everything to the Skies. We trust each other through spoken promises and vows.

"Was that your raven?" I ask.

"Yes. He brings messages to my friends."

"Are all your friends as big as you?"

He laughs loudly. "Not all. Many are on the short and stocky side."

I notice the glint of metal on his hip. Must be a weapon. "Do you fight a lot?"

"Every day."

"It's true that Paedors kill?"

"When it's needed."

"When is killing needed?"

"Ah, that's right," he says. "Skies oppose violence."

"It's just not our way." I look away when he lights up a cigarette. "We prefer silence. Peaceful things."

"Well, you don't have to fight, sweetlie. But fighting is how I survive. Otherwise I wouldn't be here to immerse myself in your gracious eyes." He smiles behind the cigarette smoke, locking his intense eyes on mine. His words are of a gentleman's nature but his build is not.

"You captivate me, Riverduna of Nameus. Is your family as lovely as you?"

I look away from his eyes when he reaches to touch my face with the back of his hand. "I have no family left," I say. "I'm alone."

"How old are you, sweetlie?"

"Seventeen. How old are you?"

He chuckles before answering. "Twenty-two."

"You look far older."

"That's what fighting does. Ages us. But we like our scars. And you seem fascinated by me too, Riverduna."

"I am," I say. "Quite fascinated."

"What would you say to a visit to Dredgar?"

"The streets?"

He runs his fingers up my neck and into my hair. "I sense your longing for adventure. You want someone to love and care for you. A best friend and partner that is more than the company of a rat or squirrel."

How does he know I talk to animals?

"You can come back here anytime you want, Riverduna. But I have a feeling that you'd like to experience another world. Another family."

"I would, Current," I say.

"And you can learn that not all Paedors are terrible people. Most of us are just a little rough around the edges."

"Your family won't try to hurt me?"

"Don't worry," he says. "Nothing bad will happen to you."

His voice is strong. His eyes resemble the night sky...sooty, inky, void of joy, but reassuring just the same.

"I'll head down first. You follow me, all right?"

I smile at Current, excited to have an adventure in Dredgar. I'll come right back up for my daily fishing expedition. But seconds into climbing down the side of a house, I feel an urge to throw up. My boots touch wet cobblestone. *What is that awful stench?*

"Sweetlie, come on. We have to hurry!"

I look down into a crimson puddle and see my distorted reflection. *Blood.* I'm standing in blood.

4

Dunn

The spoon's handle stings against my palm as I take another bite of my burnt morning porridge. Last night's fight ended with a razor blade tearing through my skin. Scars everywhere, but at least I still have my hands. Many Paedors don't. Even Tempest had gotten herself into a brawl that left her with three less fingers.

"Too quiet outside," I mutter to the brass beetle roaming past my bowl. I put out my other hand to stop it from falling off the table's edge and turn it around to skitter the other way. But the toy falters. Needs to be wound again. "I should name this one." I glance over at Katlene in her cradle. "Or I'll wait until you're able to name all your toys on your own, Katy."

I'm still eating porridge when Tempest lets herself into the house. She sets a frilly bag on the rocking chair and rushes over to me. "Let me heat up another bowl for you, Dunn. That one was burnt."

"It was. Because I made it."

"I'll make some more."

"No time," I say. "I've gotta go." I check that Katlene is still awake in her cradle before standing in front of Mama's vintage mirror and studying the thin cut on my neck that I gave myself last night. Not a

16

black eye like I promised Coald. But Current will appreciate seeing any fresh injury on me.

It might not be enough. With my eyes still on my reflection, I slide my hand into my pocket and pull out my emergency blade. I hold it parallel to my face, lightly rubbing my thumb along its edge. I know he'd like to see more damage.

"Don't you dare." Tempest swipes the knife from me with her gnarled fingers. "Stand tall while you got breath left, Duncan. Current won't be satisfied until he's got you in the ground."

"Give it back."

"Only if you promise not to add more scars today."

"If I come home tonight with any wounds, you can trust it's from the fights, and not my own hand."

"Good. Your mother told me you were too much of a people pleaser, and unfortunately she was right." She hands the blade back to me with a mischievous grin. The fire she has in her elderly bones is astounding. "Kick their asses, boy. I'll place a bet with Anglaus that you win in three hits tonight."

"Nah," I say, looking back at the mirror. "Make it one."

* * *

I look behind and above me as I step onto the cobblestone. Being a champion fighter has led me to be a constant target of spontaneous attacks by young children who are just learning to throw punches and kicks. There is no shame in the streets. Pissing, drinking, smoking, getting high off any substance that can be found. Always running into bouts of trouble among friends and strangers alike. The men of Dredgar may be tougher than the women in some regards, but in others...

"Hey! You're not crossing here, Dunn!"

Ugh. Anglaus. Three peppery-haired women take aim at me with their cannon-shotgun, eyes wild and voices raucous.

"Yeah, Dunn! You dream of kissing and overtaking all of us!"

"Why don't you look back, Ravaboy? You know you want a long look at us!"

I raise my hands as I walk on, calling back to their leader, "Wouldn't dream of it, Sashae. Keep that sassy talking up and Cure will send his own rain of bullets on your clubhouse."

"It's not a clubhouse, you idiot! It's a converted ballroom."

It never helps to stir that lot up. Yet, I can't help being humored by their responses. If I've learned anything from Tempest and Anglaus, it's that the women of Dredgar can really hold their own.

5

Riverduna

"Ferrelium," Current whispers in a raspy voice. He pulls me close as we walk into a narrow alley. "Listen, if anyone asks where you came from, tell them I saved you from an attack in the streets. You were confused after drinking too much."

"Why?"

"Don't say you're from Nameus. Only my family can know."

I notice his rapid breath. He won't stop looking to the left of us down the dark alley. "Your survival depends on me, Riverduna. Be vigilant."

"Is there always so much blood in the street?"

"This was a recent killing. Done by Ferrelium."

"Who's that?"

"Infamous gang. They use double-edged swords instead of guns."

I'm not sure how guns work, but I've always thought swords looked more elegant. I want to ask more about this sword-wielding gang, but Current's leaning against the wall, eyes focused on the street. We watch a family of four sprint past us before he looks back down at me.

"Trouble's coming, sweetlie."

"What's wrong?"

"We worry when it's silent."

How come? I think. I look up into his face, searching for a hint about what is going on.

"Because," he says, his breath becoming shallow, "that's when an ambush happens."

Before I can respond, a boar-sized force charges in, throwing us apart, and Current is out on the street yelling obscenities at his attacker. He's holding his gun to the swordsman's face, but he's not pulling the trigger.

"You guys are bloody hornets! I told you to stay off my back!"

I watch him turn the gun in his hand and swing it like a short blade. He's suddenly caught up in a messy duel, and I notice three more attackers surround Current, blocking my view of him.

"Hey, Recluse!" A boy shouts from the other side of the street. He's standing with several other children, all of them appearing to be entertained by the fight. "The girl doesn't carry a weapon!"

Recluse, the swordsman who's supposed to be keeping Current busy, turns his eyes to me. "Little Sky."

I back away as he approaches, looking up at the rooftops. *Can I climb faster than him?*

"C'mere, girl," Recluse says. "Ferrelium's better than the Ravabrigs. We'll take care of you."

Where are the short guys that Current was talking about? All of these Paedors are just as tall as he his... impossible to run from. *What are Ravabrigs?*

"What are you afraid of, little Sky?" He creeps forward on the cobblestone like a hungry spider, sword drawn and pointed at me. "You'd be better off with me than with that treacherous Current."

The children are still watching from the opposite side, half of them cheering for Current and the other half cheering for this lanky swordsman.

"Current!" I yell, hoping he'll see me, and I run to the nearest house to try to climb up the wall.

"You're mine, Sky," Recluse growls.

He throws his arm around my throat, pulling me to the ground. "I'm makin' you a woman of Ferrelium."

I struggle to breathe as his weight comes down on me. I try again to scream Current's name but I can barely hear my own voice. *Where is he? Nothing bad will happen. Did they kill him? Current!*

6

Dunn

"What a month to try to quit," I groan. I force myself to choose gum over a cigarette as I move down the street, but I hold the unlit cigarette in my fingers, comforted by the feel of the dry, grainy paper. Clangs of swords and cursing shift my attention and I look the other way. *Great day for a skirmish between a beefy Ravabrig and a mob of Ferrelium.*

I'm used to seeing Current pick fights for no reason other than showing off his brute strength. The children are definitely enjoying this drama. But there's a girl pinned under Recluse… she's panicking more than fighting. No weapons on her. And she is dressed in Sky clothing. *But she can't be a Sky. Skies never come to the streets. Is she drunk? Maybe she's mentally damaged.*

I glance down to make sure my brass spiked rings are turned the right way on my knuckles. I bring a hand to my mouth, feeling the sharpness of my metal incisors. *Look out, Recluse. This girl's not gonna be violated on my watch.* I calmly walk toward him, feeling the eyes of the street children on me, and I shout out, "HEY!"

Recluse immediately throws a look over his shoulder, taking his knee off the girl's chest. "She's mine, Dunn. Go help Current beat up my brothers while I finish her off."

"Oh, you mean drag her into your perverted sanctum of slavery and torment? Trapped in a filthy hole surrounded by rat piss and dog feces? Where there's no good-looking men for her to swoon over?"

"Shut your mouth! You Ravabrigs aren't any better than we are."

"I'm not a Ravabrig! Not like the rest of them."

He turns his back on the girl, angrily huffing as he stomps up to me, looking down into my eye. "Then what, Dunn? What do you call yourself?"

I peer around him, seeing the girl still lying on the ground, appearing too frightened to move. I look back up at him. "I'm just a fighter." And with that, I swing a fist toward his abdomen, catching fabric and skin on my spiked rings. Recluse comes back at me, too late in realizing that he's left his sword in the street. He's all anger and no focus.

"Grab his sword, darlie!" I yell at the girl. I point to where it is while ducking and dodging Recluse's strikes. But she just stares at me. Her sweaty red curls are falling in her brown eyes as she tries to stand up without shaking. "Darlie!" I yell again to her. I take a kick to the shoulder while navigating around Recluse. "Darlie, get the sword! His sword's right there!"

But she doesn't move.

"Ferrelium ass!" I spit at Recluse. He's not near as muscular as Current, but he's just as tall. If he grips me by the throat I know he'll gladly throw me down and body slam me into the cobblestone. *Bruising either way, but what else is new?*

"Hey, Rec, I wouldn't mess with that brother of mine."

Recluse and I look to where the voice came from. Current's walking toward us, blood on his shirt and trousers. Two young Ferreliums are motionless on the ground behind him, their swords sticking out of their chests.

"You good, Dunn?"

I look up at Recluse who's lowering his head like a nervous puppy, and back at Current who just asked me the question. "I'm fine," I say. "Just helping out a vulnerable girl, Cure."

"I know," he says, his eyes not leaving Recluse's face. "Get out of here, Duncan. The girl's safe with me."

"All right." I want to ask Current how he knows the girl and why she's wearing Sky clothes amidst dirty business with the Paedors, but I have to meet Vilho at the pit for my fight practice.

"Dunn!" As if on cue, Vilho is calling my name from down the street. "Dunn, the Garwin boy's been found! The mother asks for you!"

How timely. I can only pray that this one's alive.

7

Riverduna

My heart is pounding so loud that I can't hear anything. I see Current and Recluse shoving each other with angry faces, but no weapons are drawn. The one who saved me, the much shorter Paedor, is running away from the fight. I think I heard Current call him 'Dunn'. His long black hair and grey-blue eye were so different from Current's short hair and dark eyes.

"River?"

I look up at Current.

"River, are you okay?"

"He saved me."

"What?"

I stand up, holding onto Current for balance. "That Paedor. He saved me."

"That was Dunn. A friend of mine. And, lucky for you, he is the champion fighter of Dredgar."

"You promised nothing bad would happen."

Current takes a step back from me and spreads his arms. "Look where we are. This is Dredgar." But seeing the fear in my face, he comes close again, and whispers, "I won't let anyone else touch you, sweetlie. I promise."

"What do we do now?"

"I'm taking you to meet my family. They'll be excited to see you."

I look up at the rooftops as he pulls me to follow him. "When do I go back to Nameus?"

"It's not safe right now. You'll be targeted by killers if you go up." He puts his arm around my shoulders, reminding me how massive he is compared to me. "We need to get you in Paedor clothes."

"Why?"

"To blend in. You ask for an adventure and you get one, Riverduna of Nameus. Welcome to the streets."

* * *

The walk to Current's house is only a few minutes, but I'm uncomfortable the entire time, feeling exposed on the ground. The fog has completely lifted and the Paedors are creating commotion around me. It's not the same as listening to it from a distance. There's nowhere to hide down here.

"Come on," Current says. He gently nudges me ahead of him when we reach the entrance of his home, and immediately I feel a rush of unbearable warmth. It's smoky, dirty, so cramped in this space.

"Mother, this is Riverduna."

"Hi, darling. I'm Melnie." The woman by the wood stove smiles at me as if I have always belonged here. The circle of blonde braids on the top of her head remind me of Mama's hairstyle. But she is certainly a Paedor... wearing a wide dress skirt and showing bruises on her neck... just another Paedor who loves picking ugly fights.

"It's unruly out there, isn't it? Getting her a change of clothing, Cure?"

"I am. I'm going to introduce her to the boys at the Brigehouse."

The Brigehouse? I look up at Current. He returns my questioning glance with a half-smile.

"Go on upstairs to our room then," Melnie says. "Your father's out doing target practice with Warren."

"Thanks. Come, sweetlie. Third floor."

I slowly walk ahead of him, feeling more comfortable as we go higher up the stairs. "Do you have an attic on the fourth floor?"

"Yes. But there's nothing in it. Third floor's the closest you're gonna get to the rooftop, River."

As we go up, I notice framed art on the wall. All hand-drawn pictures. "Did you make these, Current?"

"My brother and I did when we were little. Mother saves everything."

The thought of him being a little boy almost makes me smile. "That's sweet of her."

"Yeah."

He beckons with a finger for me to follow him into the room, and I watch him go to a closet and fling articles of clothing on the bed.

"You can change behind Mother's screen," he says.

I hesitate to pick up the garments, but I do so as he stares at me. "You're not going downstairs?"

"No." He shrugs and sits on the edge of his parents' bed. "Go on, sweetlie. You have privacy."

All right, I think. *He's a rough-edged gentleman.* The bedroom is narrow. Hardly enough space for the lovely polished chest of drawers and full-length mirror in the opposite corner. I wonder where Current's room is. "Your mother doesn't mind sharing her clothing?"

"She offers graciously. But they may fall a bit big on you."

I peek around the wobbly partition, seeing him sitting further back on the bed with a playful grin.

"And the skirt is worn over the trousers?" I ask.

"Yes. More layers means more protection on the streets."

I struggle to untangle my hair from the buttons at the blouse collar.

The whole ensemble is itchy, hot, terribly encumbering. I look down at my former clothes piled around my feet and swallow a grumble. *I'm a nimble Sky in tawdry Paedor garb. Ugh.* I would fare better in a fight with a plain shirt and trousers. "Isn't it better for a woman to dress light and agile?"

"No. No, you're to blend in." He comes behind me, placing his fingers over mine, guiding me to secure the last button. "A woman like you will always succumb to the darkness of Dredgar." He draws in a breath, seeming all too pleased to tell me how it works. "Cannibalism. Slave brides. Torture rooms. But you can survive if you learn our way of life."

"But Skies don't want to fight."

"I know," he says, circling me as a I step out from behind the partition. "You're sweet. Agreeable." He leans in, breathing heavy on my neck, and turns me to face the mirror. "Look at yourself, Riverduna. Pure. Kissable. Not a single scar." He growls like a dog and whispers in my ear, "I'm glad I found you."

8

Dunn

I run ahead of Vilho, rushing toward the Garwin family's house. Terrible wailing is coming from inside.

"Dunn, no!" Vilho yanks on my arm as I reach for the door.

"What are you doing? You said she asked for me!"

"Don't go in there."

"Why? I have to see the boy."

"He's dead, Dunn."

I stop trying to push Vilho away. He's looking nervously past me. "What?"

"I'm sorry. They said they wanted to talk to you but I don't know why."

"Forest's dead? What happened to him?"

"The father withheld information about the Culmordi leader. One of the Ravabrigs…" Vilho trails off, clearly not wanting to say anything more.

Ravabrigs. I shake my head as I go to the door. *Of course they did it.*

"Your gang killed him! You killed him, Dunn!" The mother runs toward me, sobbing hysterically and trying to talk at the same time. "I lost two daughters to Ferrelium. And now my son's gone." She flings a bronze pendant at my face. "You taught him to fight! I hope you're slaughtered in the pit! I hope they kill you!"

Her husband wraps his arms around her, dragging her back into the house. His eyes are nothing but raw grief as he closes the door. I'm certain he's holding himself back from punching me.

I let my hair cover my eye as I start a slow walk to the fight pit. Cold water drips onto my face, the sensation relaxing my anxiety, and I glance up to see one of the suspended buckets leaking. Dredgar's water system has always fascinated me. I don't know how the other districts in Urchassi do it, but the moisture from rain and fog is collected and stored in the buckets overhead. It involves some type of lever and cable configuration which I wish I had invented, but everything I try to build just ends up in a burn or scrap pile. *Just like the Garwin boy.*

I silently take a cigarette from my pocket.

"Thought you were quitting," Vilho says as he offers a lighter.

"Do me a favor, Vilho." I look at the ground as I draw in a breath and hold it.

"Yeah?" He stays in step with me, waiting for me to continue.

I lift my head and calmly blow out a swirl of smoke. I watch it rise and dissipate into the gritty air around us. "Don't call me out on my bad habits when I'm being accused of murder."

"You didn't murder Forest. I know you treat the children better than anyone out here."

"I don't do anything to stop the violence, do I?" I try to keep my voice calm. "I perpetuate it."

"But your job is to fight. That's all you have." Vilho shrugs when I give him an annoyed look. "C'mon, man, it's all we Paedors got."

That can't be all of it. Fighting can't be the only thing we live for.

"What's that, Dunn?" Vilho is pointing to the pendant that I'm mindlessly playing with in my hand.

"Scarab beetle. Made it three weeks ago on the little guy's birthday.

He wanted one just like mine." I touch my neck where the chain should be. "Haven't worn it in a while."

"You used to wear your beetle necklace all the time."

"Yeah." I half-smile and put it in my pocket before climbing down into the pit. "Gonna bring me a drink, Vil?"

"I'll mix something together for ya." He stands at the edge and lights his own cigarette. "Harna's got a full bar again thanks to the southern imports."

"Glad your wife has ties outside Dredgar." I position myself against one wall of the pit to practice my kicks and block stances. "I'll be waiting."

"Right. I'll be back, Dunn."

Tempest would be furious if she knew I was smoking again. But I know she would also want me to cope with my guilt in a neutral, nonviolent way. If she can sit around getting tipsy with Anglaus, then I can do what makes me feel good.

"Hey, Dunn!" a passerby calls out. He's walking his bicycle around the edge of the pit, grinning down at me. "Good luck tonight. My daughters are making biscuits for you if you win."

I give him a thumbs-up, not wanting to break my concentration in practice.

"One hit. Take him down in one hit."

"I'll try," I mutter, punching the hard dirt wall. "I'll break his nose."

9

Riverduna

"Let's go downstairs, River. My mother can make us tea before we go to the Brigehouse."

I lift the front of my skirt with one hand, unable to imagine running in one, but I follow Current. "I don't think I'll get used to these clothes."

"You will. Give it time," Current says. "Mother, do you have any chamomile?"

"I just made some," Melnie says. She gestures to a cup on the table and smiles at me. "Go on, darling."

I take a step toward the table and Current is suddenly shouting. "Down! Down, Riverduna!"

"What?"

"Get down!" he says.

Melnie quickly pulls me to crawl under the table and I look at Current who's running past the stairs.

"Don't worry," Melnie reassures me. "This is our normal."

"What's going on? Why do we have to hide?"

"Current!" A voice from outside yells. "Current, the Culmordis!"

"I see 'em!" Current yells back. He's crouched down beneath a window, holding a massive gun. He looks at me and his mother under the table and motions for us to stay there.

"Culmordi?" I ask Melnie.

"Cannibals. They don't leave this district without a victim."

Gunshots explode outside and glass shatters everywhere. Current shoots through the window, his defensive fight stance impressing me. He looks like he'd let nothing get past him.

This is normal for Paedors, by how can I get used to this?

"Father!" Current calls out, "we've run them off! Let the young ones go!"

Melnie takes my hand as we get out from under the table, guiding me around the broken glass. I've never witnessed guns or their destruction. It's volatile.

"You good?" Current asks. He flicks a piece of glass from his shoulder as he comes back to me. "This happens a lot more than any of us would like."

I nod. "I'm okay."

A man resembling an older version of Current walks into the house with a muddy shirt and coat. His straw-yellow hair is spiky like a hedgehog and dotted with dark grey streaks. He's setting his long gun down while staring at me.

"Riverduna," Current says, "this is Amos. My father."

"Breathtaking girl," Amos says. He walks up to me, forcing me to tilt my head to look into his eyes. "Is my boy keeping you safe?"

"He is. And his friend Dunn is too."

"Dunn?"

"I'm the one who saved her," Current says. "Dunn just happened to walk by the fight."

Amos nods. "Ferrelium?"

"Yeah. Recluse was on top of her."

Both Amos and Current stare intently at me and I look away. I don't want to relive the attack right now.

"Introduce her to the boys. Then she can see how well-protected she is in our family."

"I'm bringing her there now," Current says. "We'll make it back before dinner."

"Good." Amos takes a seat at the table and motions for Melnie to approach. "Whiskey, dearest."

Whiskey. Alcohol. I hear rumors that Paedors drank a lot. I watch Melnie pour a glass for her husband and he drinks it one gulp.

"The Ravabrigs will love you," Current says to me. He keeps me pressed against his side as we go outside, and I find myself constantly looking left and right when we move through a section of alleys. The smell is awful. People are shouting to each other through windows and tossing various food scraps and liquids down the sides of buildings. Homes are scattered among dimly lit shops, and I can't tell any of them apart. Once every few steps we turn into an open patch of dirt and I see a giant crater in the center. Current tells me they are for the organized nightly fights.

"Everything is so close together here," I say. "Like a maze."

"Paedors make use of every alley and building. Some businesses are run out of homes."

"Do you fight over who owns the buildings?"

"All the time."

"So, who owns the Brigehouse?"

"Ravabrigs. My gang."

He sounds so confident and proud when speaking about his gang. I didn't think gangs were made of good men. "How many gangs are there?"

"Three."

"Do the gangs do anything else other than fight with each other?"

"Sure we do," he says with a grin. "Ravabrigs are the leaders of Dredgar. We keep everyone else in line."

"So, you're the good guys?"

"That depends on what side you're on, sweetlie." He pauses near a stubby red building that looks out of place surrounded by four story homes, and leans in, brushing his lips against my hair. A tingly warmth rises in my stomach when he locks his fingers in mine. "This is my second family," he says as he twists a key in the door. "You're going to learn everything about my brethren."

* * *

Bramy is the first Ravabrig I meet, and I'm immediately curious of his origin story. He looks nothing like the others... like he's lived his whole life in the sun - though there isn't any sun here that I can see. Scars cover his face, and thick black hair grows only on the right side of his head.

Separately I can see that the Ravabrigs vary in personality and age, but observing fifteen of them altogether in a small room makes me think of a band of angry pirates who lost their ship. Their voices are gentle when they speak to me, but they all have a gun on their hip and a bottle of alcohol in their hand. A few of them, with bright eyes and youthful posture, appear to be teenagers like me.

I point to the corner where two dark-complexioned Ravabrigs are flinging cards at each other on a metal table. "Is that your raven Illdam?"

"Yes. The youngest here, Enbraet and Hywill, look after him for me."

"Do you train other birds?"

"Only ravens. They make the best messengers."

"Cure," Bramy says, "where's your brother been? Haven't seen him in several days."

"Warren's spending more time on his own. Says he wants to live in the eastern district."

A burst of laughter comes from Enbraet and Hywill. "He's an idiot.

He'll be dead within a week of moving there."

"Perhaps you should be focusing on your own survival," Current says. He walks over to them and pulls out a knife, waving it in front of their faces. "Focus on avoiding my temper. And stop insulting my brother. He can take care of himself."

"You wouldn't cut us in front of your girl. She's too precious for your violence."

"She will be a Ravabrig. She'll learn how to fight just like we do." Current looks at me and grins. "Learn how to defend me and my boys on the streets. Won't you, Riverduna?"

I spin around, feeling the eyes of all sixteen of them. They're all wearing a slight smile. "I don't need to fight if you protect me."

"But you will," Bramy says. He sits down in a corner chair, cigar in his mouth. "You'll master the Ravabrig world."

"I can't imagine killing anyone for pleasure."

"No. It's not about pleasure," Current says. "It's about loyalty. And we must show loyalty to my parents as well."

Loyalty, I think. *But I am loyal to the rooftops and to the Skies.*

"I'll be back here tomorrow. Come, River. I think you've had enough introductions for the day."

Current sounds anxious. He's not stopped pacing the room since we entered. I follow him out, looking over my shoulder at the Ravabrigs. They seem kind. But I know I saw Current kill on the streets. He killed to protect me. *At least I'm not alone anymore. I can talk to all these Paedors and they seem to like talking to me.*

"Listen, sweetlie, the later it gets, the more dangers reveal themselves. From now on, you have to be settled inside my home just before dusk."

"Close to six o'clock then?"

"Yes. How do you know proper time?"

"You don't think Skies are smart? I know about clocks."

"Oh." He chuckles as we walk together. "There is a lot I will learn about you then too, isn't there?"

"Yes." I smile at the light-hearted tone in his voice. "I'd be happy to teach you about my world." *My world in Nameus. My animals friends. The photographs and children's books.* I touch my thigh, feeling the edge of a photograph I'd slipped into my trousers under the skirt. I wonder what Current will think of it. What he will think of my plushies in the attic.

10

Dunn

"Here, bud," Vilho calls.

I catch the bottle of whiskey, surprised that it's not a mix of tar and rum like he usually gives me. "Thanks, Vil. More than I need but it'll do."

He sits on the edge of the pit with his own glass bottle. "I saw you were talking to Current earlier. Looked like quite the bloody mess behind him."

"He took out two Ferreliums with their own swords."

"Again? What'd they do to deserve that?"

I throw a punch at my shadow. "They were trying to steal his girl."

"Current has another girl? He's never kept a girl alive for more than two weeks."

"Well, I don't know how he found this one. She looked very shaky."

"Probably drunk."

"Yeah." I throw another punch, smashing my fist harder into the tightly packed dirt. "That's what I thought. But she was cute."

"Yeah? How cute?"

"Cuter than what I've seen on the streets lately. The sort of sweetheart that you only find by a stroke of luck."

"Or by accident," Vilho says. "Which is how I got to be with Harna."

I can hear Vilho rambling on about his wife and I can't help but smile when I picture the attacked girl's face. I wish I had gotten her name. "She was petite," I say. "Most women around here match me in muscle and tower over my head like Greek goddesses."

"So, this one was built like a Celtic fairy instead?"

"Sweet eyes and the long red curls. Definitely a Celtic air about her."

Vilho laughs as I climb up the ladder. "Listen to you, Dunn. Goin' on about a pretty girl when you spew hate talk at the eligible women who offer kisses after your fights."

"Your wife is one of those women who flirts with me, Vilho. Better rein her in."

"Nah." He clicks his bottle to mine. "She wouldn't betray me like that. She only blows kisses when she's full of wine."

"Yeah," I say. "Which is at every fight. She's always hollering in the front of the crowd."

"I know she's crazy." He falls backward, holding the bottle against his chest. "That's why I love her."

I stand at the top of the ladder, setting my whiskey on the ground. "The girl I want is always taken by a jerk."

"You mean by Current."

I shrug. "Not refuting that statement."

"Why not try fighting for the one he's got now."

"You're shitting me, Vilho."

He belches and rolls to his side. "I'm being serious."

"You know what happens whenever I pick a fight with him."

"How about instead of the physical ass-kicking, you attempt a mind-blowing takedown?"

"Elaborate," I say.

"Win her over with subtle movements. And you do it right under Current's nose. He may be the boss of you and the Ravabrigs, but no way in hell should the man control who or what you crave. Take the girl for yourself."

"No way." I slide back down into the pit. "I'll lose the other eye and possibly my entire face."

"You have the same level of smarts as Current. The game is even."

"He is always one step ahead of me. All the Ravabrigs are."

"Not if you keep your poker face." Vilho leans over the edge on his stomach, holding both bottles of whiskey. "You know how to look and where to look to make your opponents think they've won. You can use the same trick on the boss."

"Stop tempting me."

"Dunn, you keep slipping back into a stupid smile. You're thinking about her and you don't even know her name."

"It's pointless," I say. "It's pointless to try to get her."

"Why?"

"Cure's already sprung his trap. By the time he's done with that girl, she won't want anything to do with another man."

<h1 style="text-align:center">11</h1>

<h1 style="text-align:center">Riverduna</h1>

Current's little brother hasn't stopped talking since he entered the house. I'm sitting between Current and Amos and we are all watching thirteen-year-old Warren enthusiastically shovel food into his mouth while telling a story with wild arm gestures. I've not seen this much food on a table in my whole life. A working man's type of meal. Paedors must burn lots of calories in their fights in order to eat all this.

"That's pork stew."

Warren points at my bowl. I haven't eaten any of it yet.

"You never had pork before?"

"No. I just catch fish off the roof." I dip my spoon in my dish and bring some broth to my mouth. "I walk to the southern river and catch and cook it over a fire."

"All our meat is imported," Warren says. He takes a piece of bread and puts the whole thing in his mouth, still managing to speak around his chewing. "From the other districts."

"That's a long way to walk, darling," Melnie says to me, talking over Warren's comment.

"I don't mind. I love living up there." I wait for her to respond or at least give me a smile of acknowledgment, but she just drops her head

41

and returns to silently eating her stew.

For a moment there is no sound except for obnoxious chewing and utensils clinking against dishes. Eventually I notice Amos pushing his plate forward. He scoots his chair back, and without any communication, Melnie quickly stands and brings him a glass of whiskey. Then she sets a full glass in front of Current.

"I haven't seen a Sky girl among us in years. Why'd it take so long for you to find one, Current?"

Current seems bothered by his father's question, and now I'm also concerned. I turn to Amos. "You were looking for me?"

Amos looks right at Current, continuing to talk as if he hadn't heard me. "I was going to say that your taste in females had gone terrible, but seeing Riverduna makes up for the others you brought home."

"That's an irrelevant statement, Father," Current says.

But why? They were looking for Skies? "Why were you trying to find a Sky girl?"

"Skies have been targets of the Culmordis and Ferrelium for years. Our family's made it a mission to save as many of your people as we can."

"The danger is invisible to you," Melnie says in a soft voice. "Current led you down before they got to you first. And now you will learn to be a strong Paedor woman."

"But I'm not a Paedor."

"Oh, c'mon!" Warren hollers. "You'll be just like the rest of 'em in a week, Riverduna. Guaranteed!" He stands, grins smugly, and heads down the hall out of sight.

I don't know how to fight someone. I don't think I can punch or kick. Have never tried. Why would a Sky girl voluntarily become a Paedor?

"Do you want children?"

I jump at Amos's brusque voice. He's sitting close to me again, leaning toward me with a heavy breath.

"Maybe. I… I haven't thought about it."

"There is no maybe, girl."

"I don't know." I look at Current for help, but he's downing his alcohol with an intense ferocity. "I like my life as it is."

"Life doesn't go the way we want it. It would be a waste of that beauty if you didn't have any children."

"Amos!" Melnie's gentle manner switches to a gruff bark. She's rising from her chair, looking right at her husband. "Don't push her. She's seen more than enough change today."

If the choice was left solely up to me, I'd be jumping out of my chair and running out the door back to Nameus, but being flanked by two massive men isn't helping my courage. *I feel like I'm shrinking.*

"Are you taking me back up after dinner?"

"I have a better idea," Current says. "Spend one night with me in my parents' room. They said we could use it as long as you are here. I want you to listen to the Cruftetin fights."

"Is that where Dunn does his fighting?"

"Yes. He's down there now. The main pit is just behind our house."

Amos grins, lifting his glass for a sip. "You'll get used to it here, Riverduna. Plenty of Skies have ended up on the ground and made a life for themselves."

"I didn't know Skies chose to live here. We usually prefer the high ground."

"Isn't it better to be with a family than alone in the cold?"

Melnie and Amos are trading the same sort of sweet gaze that Mama and Father would give to each other. I look down, embarrassed by the tears in my eyes, and Current puts his hand over mine.

"I know you miss your parents. You'll get more comfortable with us."

"Is it true about the other gangs trying to kill Skies?"

"Yes. My father and I have worked hard to protect your people in Nameus, but the women and children are harder to track down. You are all so crafty."

"We're quiet," I say. "Silence is calming."

"Why don't you try my favorite means of calming, sweetlie," Current says as Melnie sets a cup of watery red tea in front of me. "Apple chamomile tea."

"All right." I lift the cup and look to where Amos is pacing near the fire. I can't tell in the dim light if he is smiling or scowling.

"It's good. I promise," Current says.

But I study the liquid, unsure if I like the look of the red and white swirls amidst the milky color.

"Drink and we can go up."

I drink all of it. *Pleasant fruity taste.*

* * *

Current holds my hand all the way up the stairs, pointing to the window in his parents' room. "We can hear Cruftetin from the bed, but you can also lean out and try to see their silhouettes in the fog."

I glance over my shoulder to find him casually undressing. I blush hard, turning back to the window. I touch the frame, digging my nails into the dirty corners. *Paedor men are not timid in any capacity. Where do I look?*

"Wild, isn't it?" he says.

He's being nice to me but I don't feel right.

"What are they shouting?" I ask, trying my best to ignore his naked chest touching my back.

"The names of the fighters. They're calling to Dunn now. The louder the crowd gets the more likely he is winning against his opponent."

"Can we go down to watch it?"

"I'll take you down there tomorrow. You need to rest."

I'm not getting any rest in this room. Not if he stays this close to me.

His arms are around my waist, gently pulling me against him. "There is no time to daydream here, River. One minute of being lost in your head will lead to your head being lost."

"What does that mean?"

"It means you must always keep your guard up." He gently pulls hair back from my face and presses his cheek to mine. "That is what a good fighter does. He doesn't let his opposition steal his determination to win."

I lean forward to peer further out the window, but Current's grip on me tightens. "Skies like to run, don't they? Do you like the feeling of adrenaline?"

Adrenaline. Adrenaline is freedom. Freedom on the rooftops. "Yes," I whisper. "I love adrenaline."

"Did you feel adrenaline when Recluse attacked you?"

"No. I felt fear." I shiver as a harsh wind shoots through the window. "Fear is not adrenaline."

"Adrenaline comes from fear and pleasure, Riverduna. It's a good thing to feel." Current draws me to the middle of the room, nodding toward the bed. "Wanna lie down?"

"I sleep on the floor," I say. "I want to sleep by myself."

"I won't do anything to you, River. I promise."

"I'll sleep on the floor." I push away from him, and he lets me sit on the floor.

"All right," he says softly. "Need a blanket?"

"No." I wait for him to lie down on the bed before I turn to my side and run my fingers along the floorboards. I feel the roughness of the wood. I smell the dust particles. It's not outside but it feels better to me than a pillow. It feels like an attic. *How do I get back up? How long do I have to stay here?*

12

Dunn

My third opponent of the night, an eighteen-year-old named Sorrel, wears a confident grin as he circles me. He looks into my eyes, bouncing in place like a sugar-obsessed child. I can tell that he is new to this. Unaware of my strengths. No clue as to where my power comes from.

"I've heard of you. Ravabrig slave."

He thinks I'm a slave?

"You've taken down so many fighters in Dredgar."

I keep my mouth shut. He's talking way too much.

"What's your secret, Duncan?" His eyes shift from me to the crowd. He's basking in the excited hollering of his friends.

"I heard you bled Forest out. Cut his throat."

They all think I'm a murderer. "No."

Sorrel grins wider, proud of himself for getting me to talk.

"What knife did you use? Did Bramy set the trap for the boy or did you?"

Son of a demon. I throw myself forward, ramming him against the wall. I punch, kick, bite. I do everything I've taught myself to do. I have tunnel vision.

I am not a killer. I don't kill. I defend.

I only stop beating on my cocky opponent when I hear Vilho yelling that I've won. "He's down, Dunn! Back off!"

I spit out blood between hard breaths, unable to feel any sensation in my body. No soreness yet. No idea where I've taken hits.

"Another fight lived," Vilho says as he steadies the top of the ladder. I quicken my pace once I've climbed out of the pit, hurrying to escape the crowd. I don't need praise right now.

I taste blood... but is it mine?

* * *

Tempest doesn't say a word when I come home and sit at the table. She brings a bowl of onion soup and sets it down next to a dish of hazelnuts. "I know you smoked, Dunn. I'm not gonna ask why."

"I got the Garwin boy killed."

"What motive would you have to do that? You've known Forest since he was three."

"I'm aligned with the Ravabrigs," I say. "Everyone assumes I'm just as deadly as they are."

"All right." Tempest sits across from me, sliding a brand-new pack of cigarettes on the table. "I figured this would happen," she says. "Who was on the receiving end of your wrath tonight?"

"A rookie named Sorrel. He got caught up in the cheers and trash talk. Easy to bring him down."

She grins. "One hit?"

"I don't know. I just went beast-like on him."

"Did you use your spiked rings?"

"No. That's cheating."

"But they always cheat against you."

I bite into one of the chestnuts and feel a sharp pain in my mouth. Sorrel must have hit one of my teeth. "As long as I win fairly on my end, Tempest, that's what I care about."

"Well," she says, "as long as you stay alive is what I care about. For me and Katy."

We both look at Katlene lying on the rug. She is trying her best to roll over and reach a knitted yellow ball.

"I promised Mama I'd always keep her baby girl alive. I'd do anything. You know that."

Tempest brings me a second bowl of soup and sits down again, sipping on a dusty wine bottle. "Does that mean you've given more thought to Brigandre?"

I answer her without looking up. "It won't work. I've tried."

"Then you think of a different way to get there. Imber told me about the evidence. The anarchy catalyst."

"Chaos catalyst. That's what I call it."

"You have to see it in person, Dunn."

"I can't. I'm cursed, Tempest. The dead and stolen horses, the workshop fires, the airship explosion. Clearly I'm not meant to reach Brigandre in my lifetime."

"But what if Imber was right?"

"If Mama was right," I say, looking hard into Tempest's eyes, "then all my attempts have been useless." *Dredgar will never change. Even if I found a way... this society and its people are too far gone.*

13

Riverduna

I wake up in a sweat, my body sticking to the sheets. I don't remember getting into bed. I don't feel rested. *Pain. Aching pain all over. Feverish.* It's dark in the room… dark outside the window. *What time is it?*

"River? You okay?" Current's hand is touching my face.

I peer over the edge of the bed and see a dress on the floor. The same dress I was wearing at dinner.

"River? What are you looking at?"

Feeling nauseous and breathless, I stare at a spider sitting on its web. *I'm in a cage. I want to be out. I need to go outside, to breathe.* "I feel sick, Current."

"Relax, sweetlie. Lie back down."

My legs are trembling too much to walk. I wouldn't make it to the window. But it's right there. The window's right there. But Current is stronger. "When did I get in bed?"

"An hour ago." He's kissing my ear and neck. "You just wanted to cuddle."

"But I don't remember that. I can't share a bed with you."

"You're my girl. My parents let me claim this room so we could have the bigger bed."

Current, please stop. I turn my face into the pillow, hoping he'll leave me alone. But he doesn't stop. I look at the spider again, seeing it climb up the wall. *Don't leave me, spider. Stay.*

"Look at me, Riverduna." Current forces me to look up at his face, and I hear myself whimper. "You're my girl. Got that?"

I barely nod in response. He kisses me again. His hands touch every inch of my body. And I do nothing. I just stare at the spider on the wall. I see the little critter lift two of its legs as it balances on an invisible thread.

Current's heavy breathing drowns out my own shallow, panicked breaths. *I'm in a dream world. I'm not about to throw up from the pain. I'm not gonna cry.*

14

Dunn

"I know that you slept better than I did." I look at Katlene as we both lie on the floor, grinning at her interest in the mechanical horse and centipede marching past her. "I hope you learn to make toys like me, Katy. We need another genius brain around here."

"Did you just call yourself a genius?"

I glance up at Tempest and take the lavender tea from her hand. "Why not?"

"Because," she says, walking over to the fire, "geniuses don't make good fighters. And Ravabrigs hate Paedors who think for themselves."

"Exactly why I'm on Current's bad side," I say. I sit up to drink my tea and grin at Tempest.

"Current is nothing but bad sides."

"Agreed. But we have a complex history."

"There's nothing complex about your friendship. You'll get yourself killed if you stray further out of line."

I think about tying my hair back today but decide not to. I look more intimidating with it hanging down, trapping all the dirt and sweat. "Some of the boys appreciate me."

"Yes." Tempest picks Katlene up and sits with her in the rocking chair.

"I saw Bramy's face when he watched Esann's execution. He was the only one who had tears in his eyes. He's got a weakness."

"Everyone has a weakness, Tempest. Doesn't mean he's any less loyal to the boss."

"Oh, please. I wish you didn't view Current as your boss."

"His family created the Ravabrigs. I owe my success in Cruftetin to him." *And yet... Current is such a curse.*

"Well, I'll see you back home tonight," Tempest says. "Good luck on the practice and fights."

"Thanks. Don't worry about dinner for me tonight. I'll be at Current's house."

"What?" Tempest stops me from opening the door. "Since when do you eat meals with his family?"

"I know it's been a few months since I've accepted their offer."

"What's the lure?" she asks with a smile. "His new girl?"

"How did you know about his girl?"

"It's all over the streets." She and I both look at Katlene, who's babbling. "Anglaus and I spread all the gossip."

"Very helpful," I say with an eye roll.

"Yes, I am helpful. I play a very important part in the information system."

"How come you ladies never find something else to do besides chat about the rest of us?"

Tempest answers me as I stand outside the open door. "The nature of a female, Duncan, is to tell any and all secrets."

"And what makes you think Current's girl is a secret?"

"I don't think she is," Tempest says in a coarse whisper. "But I think he's keeping her from you."

That girl, I think. *She's his next wife.*

I walk down the cobblestone, trying to narrow my thoughts to the taste of blood and mud. But all I can think of now is the girl I saved from being violated. *I saved her from the wrong man.*

53

15

Riverduna

Bramy and Current are excited that I know how to read and write cursive. I'm put to work penciling down a mix of numbers and circular symbols inside the Brigehouse, and despite still feeling tired, I don't mind having something to do. Anything to keep Current from putting his hands all over me.

"What are these for?" I ask.

"It's a code for our gang. Only a Ravabrig can understand it."

"Do I get to learn it?"

Current sets a glass of whiskey on the table. "Not until you pass the test."

"What's the test?"

"You get drunk and punch me. Then we'll make love in front of the boys." He leans over the table, staring into my eyes, and whispers, "You've recovered from last night, haven't you, sweetlie?"

I hear laughter from Bramy and look at the amber alcohol in front of me. *My lower body hurts in a way it never has before. This shaky feeling isn't normal.* I look back up at Current and I lie. "Yes. I have."

He grins. "I thought so."

"I doubt she's telling the truth," Bramy says. "She's been wobbly ever since she came in with you."

Stop talking about me, I think.

"I'm guessing you haven't had alcohol before?"

I look at Bramy who's approaching me, then look down at the glass. "Skies don't drink that much."

"You should start," Current says. He pushes the glass right up to my pad of paper. "Now."

I meet his eyes, shoving the glass toward him. I shake my head.

"C'mon, sweetlie. Drink with me."

"Cure! Cure, get out here!"

Current snarls as we both look toward the hollering coming from outside. "Anglaus just shot at Hywill!"

"Get under the table," Current says without looking back at me. "Watch her, Bramy."

I watch Bramy carry a gun in from another room. He gives me a reassuring nod before standing against the wall.

"Another gang?" I ask him.

"Anglaus isn't a gang. It's a bloody tea party. Just a bunch of old Paedor women who like to show the men up now and then."

I flatten myself against the floor when a burst of gunfire hits the Brigehouse. *How can this happen every day? It doesn't stop.*

As much as I don't want to fight, I'm beginning to think I'll have to in order to get home. There has to be someone else to trust. Someone who doesn't cling to the oath of violence. How can a woman protect herself against these men? I've never even touched a blade or a gun, nor do I have any desire to.

16

Dunn

I pause in my descent into the pit, taking notice of a mother walking her two toddlers across the street. The bluebell flower pattern of her skirt looks like the one Mama always wore. I had told Tempest to pay Dredgar's main seamstress to stop making any clothing with that pattern.

"Dunn," Vilho says, throwing a cigarette at my head. "Dunn, I made you something."

"What is it?"

He tosses a pendant at my feet and I pick it up. "A bird?"

"It's a raven for good luck."

"Ravens belong to Current. My luck is in beetles."

"Just keep it. Every Paedor has a secret charm like this, and you've thrown away each one I've gifted to you."

"Luck doesn't always mean survival."

Vilho sighs, leaning over the edge of the pit with his cigarette in his mouth. He looks at me and then up at the street before exhaling a puff of smoke. "I know you've been thinking about Brigandre again."

"What's it to you?"

"Dunn, you leave this district without permission, and your little sister will be found dead."

"I know what's at stake. I'd be an idiot to leave without her."

"Well," Vilho says, climbing down into the pit next to me, "you'd also be dead."

"Expected," I say.

"And if you want to have a chance at Current's girl, I'd make it happen quick. There's no knowing how far he's already gone with her."

"She's probably at his house right now. I'm going over there before the fights start. I just want to see her up close. Be able to talk to her."

I go back to punching the dirt wall when Vilho starts to speak again. "Keep things civil. Promise me you won't let Amos mess with your head."

I shake my head. Vilho breaths out a swirl of smoke and silently observes my practice.

"I won't," I say. "He won't get to me this time."

"Sometimes I wish I had your passion for fighting."

"Why's that?"

"All the free alcohol."

I trade sly grins with him. "You know I don't drink all that. Most of it goes to Tempest."

"You know she probably gives it to Anglaus."

Dang it. I draw back and land a solid kick on my shadow. *She probably does give it to them. Ugh. Anglaus.*

17

Riverduna

It's taking a long time for me to put this heavy dress and makeup on. Melnie tells me it's how Paedor women dress when company comes over, but all I can think is how unflattering it looks in the mirror. *I'm not the same Riverduna.* But even though I feel uncomfortable, I also feel safer. I feel safe when Melnie is with me.

"Try some of my perfume," she says.

"Skies don't smell like fancy flowers. We prefer a natural, earthy smell."

"Just try a little. Dunn will be here any minute."

Dunn's coming to the house? "Current's friend?"

"Yes. He's been a friend to our family for years. We used to have dinner with his parents every night."

I groan as Melnie takes her time adjusting the sleeves of my dress. It's way too lacy.

"I don't like how this feels, Melnie."

"You'll get used to it. You're one of the family now, River."

I don't want to be upset with this woman. She's been so nice to me. But looking at myself next to her in the mirror, I feel nervous. *I don't belong in the family.*

"Wow, sweetlie, you're gorgeous!" Current exclaims from outside the door.

I meet him at the top of the stairs and after Melnie heads down, I walk beside him, trying my best not to stumble in the long skirt. *This feels so strange.*

"Dunn," Current calls to his friend standing at the bottom floor, "I don't believe you caught this girl's name before."

Dunn smiles at me. "I did not."

I smile back, and Current's arm tightens around my waist. "This is Riverduna," he says.

"Riverduna," Dunn repeats. He looks me up and down. "Is that one of Melnie's dresses?"

"Current said the blue lace looks good with my hair."

"He's right," Dunn says. He's still smiling at me and I feel my face growing hot. "It's perfect for you."

"That's more than enough flattery, Duncan," Current grumbles. "Come on. You can sit where Warren usually does."

Dunn looks surprised as he takes his place at the table, directly across from me. "Where's he off to?"

"Shooting with friends. You know how he likes to stir trouble."

"Of course," Dunn agrees. "We all do." He chooses the smallest portion of chicken to put on his plate. It amuses me to see him acting so polite when other Paedor men are openly feral.

Amos is sitting at the head of the table, but I notice Dunn doesn't acknowledge his presence.

"What district are you from, River?"

Dunn's one eye is staring intensely at me as I try not to look at Current. He made sure I memorized all the answers. *How did he know what Dunn would ask me?*

"I'm an orphan," I lie. "From this district. Dredgar."

"Do you normally dress like a Sky?"

"I woke up drunk in an alley. My clothes were stolen so I had to wear anything I could find."

Amos chuckles and I watch Current down two glasses of whiskey. Dunn's not drinking alcohol. He just sips the tea that Melnie quietly brought him.

"You have a gun, right? Every Paedor has one. Especially the women."

"Well…" I glance up at Current's face and he frowns. "Sometimes I get carried away with drinking and forget to bring a weapon with me. I didn't have parents to teach me to fight."

"How often do you drink?" Dunn asks.

Okay. I have to prove my point to everyone at the table. I reach out and take a glass of whiskey, bringing it to my mouth. My hand is trembling as I feel the three men watching me.

"River," Current whispers. "Drink it slow."

But I take a huge gulp of it. The burning in my mouth brings tears to my eyes. But I keep it down.

"Wow," Dunn says. He drinks some of his tea, and I can see he's trying to hide a smile.

Melnie sets more bread and chicken in the center of the table and sits beside Dunn. "River's a tough girl. Just like any of us."

"Tough," Amos grunts at his wife. He shoots me a stern look before saying, "Riverduna's not learned any toughness."

"It's progress," Current says. He clears his throat, gesturing in Dunn's direction. "The cut on your neck, Dunn. Is that what you gave to yourself after you convinced Coald not to hit you?"

Dunn lowers his head as he stabs a piece of chicken with his fork. "From a fight."

"That's pathetic. You know I don't like those tricks."

Tricks? What trick is Dunn playing on Current?

"I'm only trying to watch out for the children," Dunn says.

"And that," Current says with a wave of his knife, "is why the boys make fun of you. You're too sensitive."

Isn't sensitive a good thing?

Dunn looks insulted by what Current said, but he's not yelling or picking a fight. Part of me wishes he would rise up and punch Current in the face… get even with his opponent. But Skies never desire revenge. *Why am I wanting it for him?*

18

Dunn

"Speaking of sensitive," Amos says to me, "Current tells me you've been holding back in the pit. He thinks you could be making some real kills."

"I don't strike to kill."

"You're a Ravabrig. It's been four years since you —"

I see Riverduna listening intently and rise from my chair, abruptly cutting Amos off. "No!" *She doesn't need to hear about that part of my past.*

"But you've always looked like the perfect bait for an unsuspecting victim. The perfect assassin."

Amos. Flattering me like he did when I was his helpless victim. The memories of those torture years hit me so hard in the gut that I taste vomit. "I'm not going to play that role, Amos."

"Current and I can bend the rules for you. Make things more interesting."

"I'd like to stick to the rules that already exist. Cruftetin was Vilho's idea, and I trust his boundaries."

"Vilho," Amos snorts. "He knows nothing about real fighting."

"It is real fighting," I say. I push my cup of tea aside and reach for the whiskey, staring Amos down as I drink it. The room is silent until

Current's voice breaks through the tension.

"Hey, Dunn, River and I would like to come down to watch tonight's fight."

I look at Current, irritated at seeing his arm around Riverduna. She looks uncomfortable being held against him. "Is that right? You don't mind seeing the violence, darlie?"

"Current says you're the champion." Riverduna's voice is sweet and melodic. "I want to see it for myself."

"I'd welcome another beautiful spectator," I say with a smile. "Just stay close to Current because the crowd gets rowdy."

"I will," she says. She looks at Current and he suddenly gives her an aggressive kiss. I can tell by her tense body language that she doesn't like it.

"How do you fight with that hair hanging in your face, Dunn?" Amos asks as I get up and head for the door. "Why not cut it?"

"I like my hair," I mutter. "You walking with me to the pit?" I say to Current and Riverduna.

"And the eyepatch," Amos's abrasive voice continues as he stands and approaches me. "What about showing off the glass eye that I gave you?"

"I'd rather not."

"Always combative with me, aren't you, Dunn?"

"Later, Amos," I say in my exit.

Riverduna is smiling excitedly as she follows me and Current to the pit, but all I can think of is Amos and what he's yelling out the door.

"Make me proud, boy! You're still my favorite."

I shudder as I start to run. *Favorite. I was his favorite victim. Still am. Hell.*

<h1 style="text-align:center">19</h1>

<h1 style="text-align:center">Riverduna</h1>

I can't get the taste of Current's kiss out of my mouth. Spitting is no good because he'll know why I'm doing it. But looking around at the noisy crowd gathering to watch Cruftetin, I realize I could do anything at this moment and no one would care. Half of the people are screaming at each other in broken and slurred syllables, and almost all of them look and smell like they just bathed in garbage.

"Hey."

I feel a nudge at my back and look over my shoulder. A golden-eyed woman is holding out a cigarette to me. "You need this."

"I don't smoke," I say.

"You live with Current." She points to Current whose back is turned to me. He's busy talking to Dunn and another man.

"But I don't smoke," I say again.

"Well then, Riverduna, you come find Anglaus when the beatings get worse. We'll help you out."

"Current doesn't hurt me."

"No?" She lowers her voice, speaking closer to my ear. "What about the drugging you with tea and pulling you into bed?"

I don't know how to respond. *Current did pull me into his bed. But I don't remember it happening.*

The woman lays a hand on my arm and silently gestures to the gun strapped to her hip. "Anglaus," she whispers before backing into the crowd. "Ask for Sashae."

Anglaus. The women who shot at the Brigehouse.

"River? You all right?"

I look up at Current. He's stroking my hair with a gentle hand. "Yes," I say. "I was just talking to-"

"That was Sashae. The leader of Anglaus."

"She sounds friendly."

"You can't trust her. She's been a tyrant to the Ravabrigs."

I nod at him but silently disagree. I think the women are nicer than the men. "Current," I say as we walk closer to the fight pit, "why did you have to kiss me so hard?"

"You didn't like it?"

I look away from him, choosing to not say anything else. *I really don't like it.* But then watching Dunn climb into the pit makes me feel a new kind of nervous. It looks so far down.

"First hit! Get 'em, Dunn! Take him down fast!"

"Knock him out!"

The other man in the pit has a similar build to Dunn, but his face looks meaner. They pace forward and back as the energy of the crowd intensifies.

"Watch Dunn's first move," Current says into my ear. "He's a master at this."

I feel myself drawn to the tension in the pit, the sight and smell of the dirt putting a smile on my face. I've read about so many animals in books, and Dunn reminds me of a wolverine. *Compact fierceness. The snarls.*

In one fast motion, Dunn crouches beneath the other fighter's punch and charges, wrestling him to the dirt. They hit each other again and again. I don't see blood yet. Dunn doesn't look tired.

"How long does it go on for?" I ask Current.

"As long as they are both conscious," he says.

Dunn jumps up and circles his opponent who's lying on the ground. They don't speak to each other or to the crowd. They just stare at each other.

"What's happening?"

"Just watch," Current says. "It's all part of the fight."

Then I see Dunn lift his head, gazing up at the opposite edge of the pit. He drops his arms to his sides. The other fighter starts to get up and move behind Dunn.

Dunn. Turn around! What are you doing?

"What the hell are you doing?" Current whispers. He relaxes his grip on my waist, nudging me to stand to the side of him. "Dunn! Fight!"

What's he looking at? I try to follow Dunn's eye, but I only see the raucous crowd. And Amos. Current's father Amos appearing at the front of the crowd. *Is that who Dunn is looking at?*

"Fight! Fight him, Duncan! Turn around!"

Dunn barely turns an inch when the other man pushes off from the wall and brutally kicks him in the head, sending him to the dirt.

"Dunn!" I yell out.

"He's fine. He's fine, sweetlie," Current reassures me.

"He's not getting up."

"He will. He'll stand up."

But the crowd goes silent. We all wait. We wait to see Dunn get to his feet. It feels like an hour. *He's fine. He's fine. Get up, Dunn.*

"C'mon, brother," Current says. "Don't let this be the night you fail." He presses his hand to my cheek. "Stay here." Then he jumps into the pit, running to Dunn's motionless body. "Get up. C'mon. C'mon!"

I look around and see the crowd dispersing. *Is this how a fight is supposed to end?*

"Taking him to the Brigehouse," Current says as he kneels to lift Dunn into his arms. "Wheelden's got medicine for this."

I nod, hoping that Dunn's not permanently injured.

"Drop me!" Dunn suddenly screams in a hoarse voice. He strikes out at Current. "Amos, drop me! Now! Let go of me!"

Current looks confused as he tries to hang onto Dunn. He looks up at me as I also watch Dunn's frantic behavior. *He thinks Amos is holding him? Why doesn't he recognize Current's face?*

20

Dunn

Amos is carrying me. He's trying to take me away.

"Dunn, it's me! Hey!"

"Just drop him, you fool! Let him down!"

"The fight's stopped. Get the other one out of the pit!"

I feel my body slam into the dirt, and I hear Current's panicked voice. Current never panics. *Is Amos gone?*

"Dunn, it's me. It's Current. Why'd you call me Amos?"

I wipe an arm across my mouth and shake my head. Double vision. Blood everywhere. A few teeth missing.

"Bloody hell, Duncan! Answer me! Why'd you lash out? I thought you were gone with that steel boot to the head!"

"Just give me a cigarette."

"I've never seen you trembling like this. The hallucinations come back?"

I look up at Current, motioning to his trouser pockets. "Cigarette. I need to take a few nights off."

"To do what?" Current asks as he lights it for me. "You keep us entertained."

Entertainment. I breathe out smoke and give a nod of acknowledgment to Riverduna. She looks so fragile out here. So vulnerable in the dark. "That's all I am, isn't it?" I say to Current. "That's all I do as a Ravabrig. Like a court jester forced to perform at the king's will."

"Why did you shout my father's name?"

"I saw him."

"So what? He loves watching you, brother."

I hate Amos's eyes on me. I hate how he ruins my focus. "I'm sorry I let you down, Current," I say. "But you should be thankful that I don't cheat like the others do."

"Steel-toed boots aren't cheating. Your opponent was just a seasoned fighter. Why don't you bring a weapon to the next fight? I'll let you take anything you want from the Brigehouse."

I look at Current's arm drawing Riverduna close against him. He grins and she half-smiles at me.

"No, Cure," I say. "I just need to rest."

I walk far away from the pit and sit down in an alley, smoking three cigarettes before heading home.

21

Riverduna

Back at Current's house I have a drink of tea and fall asleep on the bedroom floor. It's pitch black when I wake up in the bed. And I don't just hear Current's voice. I hear Amos too. Both of them whispering about me. I keep my face pressed against the pillow and stretch out my arm to feel for any webs. The spider. He's still there. *Is this really happening again?*

"You awake, River?"

I close my eyes at Current's raspy voice in my ear. *Get off me. Please, get off me.* But the pain starts. The aching and trembling all through my body. The dark room spins and I let out a sob. *Spider, c'mere. Sit with me. Bite me. Do anything.* I shriek when Current pulls me away from the bed's edge. I grab the pillow and hold it up to my face.

"Getting feisty," he says.

"Stop," I say. "Let me lie on the floor."

"C'mon, River. Kiss me back. C'mon."

The bed begins to move like an ocean in an earthquake and I look back toward the spot where I know the spider is watching from his web. *Caligo. I'll name you Caligo.*

"Relax, sweetlie."

What did I do to make him hurt me? What did I do wrong?

"She'll calm down," Amos says in the blackness. "All the others learned to love it."

"Yeah," Current says. He's holding my wrists as he sits on top of me. "Until they tried to run."

They are talking to each other while I'm in pain. It's as if I'm invisible or a voiceless animal.

"It's all right, River." His tone softens as he kisses my neck. I'm trying not to cry, but I know he can feel the tears on my face. "I'm teaching you to be a Paedor."

He finally gives me room to breathe, lying beside me, and I break down in uncontrollable sobs when he embraces me against him. There are no sheets, no clothes between us. Just sweat. I've never felt so sick.

22

Dunn

I fiddle with a new toy instead of falling asleep. A bronze wind-up turtle to add to Katlene's collection. We're both lying on a thick blanket near the fire, my jaw and the back of my head throbbing from where I was struck.

"So glad you don't have to see your big brother get beat up," I say. "Never a good sight."

I wish Katy was old enough to talk with me to help time pass faster. The biggest reaction I get from her is when I sing the Echo Song... she smiles and laughs.

"Duncan, you're still here?"

Tempest? Her voice startles me.

"It's morning. Aren't you supposed to be out?"

I roll over when Tempest tries to step over me to get to Katlene. "Morning? I barely slept."

"Yeah, you look really bad."

"But I didn't hear you come into the house. How long have you been here, Tempest?"

She glances down at the pocket watch she pulls from her skirt and shrugs. "It's eight now. Got in a couple hours ago."

"And you didn't wake me?"

"I didn't see you on the floor. You had this whole blanket pulled over your head."

I sit up slowly with a groan. "I gotta get to the Brigehouse. Skipping practice today."

"Why?"

"I need to make another effort with them. The Ravabrigs are the reason I have this house."

"Not in my book, Dunn. But try not to get kicked in the head again, would you? I swear one day you will come home with irreversible brain damage."

I take a sip of the black coffee that Tempest hands me. "Did Sashae tell you about that?"

"Nothing gets past her. Stay well out there, boy."

"I'll do my best, Tempest," I say. But looking out the window I see children running down the street with swords in hand, and I think about who they're going to stab them with. *Maybe me.* Current will threaten them if they refuse to stand with the Ravabrigs. Like it or not, I should get on better terms with him.

* * *

I find I'm only one of three Ravabrigs present at the Brigehouse. The boys like to sleep in most of the time. But it's not just me, Bramy, and Raelot in here. Riverduna is sitting at a corner table writing something. Her hair is pulled back in a messy bun and I can see her nervously tapping her foot, causing the whole table to rattle. It was clearly a bad night for her too.

Sorting through an old stash of wine in the back room, I pick out a bottle and two glasses, bringing it to the table.

"This goes down easier than whiskey, darlie," I say as I pour it. "Try it."

Riverduna looks at me, says nothing, and returns to writing.

"It's safe to drink. My family's nanny Tempest gifted it to us a few years ago, but wine stays good for a while."

She puts her pen down and watches me take a drink of it. "Current says I have to get drunk in front of the Ravabrigs."

"You don't have to." I sit across from her. "Anything you drink here I'll drink with you. Okay?"

"Okay." She looks at me and at the glass of red wine. It takes a minute for her to pick it up and have a sip, but she finally does. "It doesn't burn as much," she says.

"Yeah." I keep my voice even with hers, ignoring the stares from Bramy and Raelot. They'll be telling Current all about this interaction.

"You're not like Current," she says.

"I'm not like anyone." I lean in to meet her eyes with mine. "I'm myself. I'm Duncan."

"You are," she says. "You're very kind to me."

I grin when she shows a small smile, and in the softest of whispers I say, "I respect your honor, Riverduna. No lie."

23

Riverduna

Dunn's presence is calming. It's so different from the other people in Dredgar. He doesn't scowl and glower or speak with a boisterous tone.

"Hey, Dunn." Current comes through the door with a couple more of the boys. "Didn't think I'd see you join us for a meeting. What's the occasion?"

"I'm a Ravabrig, aren't I?" Dunn says.

Current grins and pulls out a crumpled piece of paper, holding it up to the room. "New message. I'd ask someone else to read it but not one of you takes the time to learn." He looks in my direction, silently signaling me to put my eyes back down on my work. "Now all of you listen to me." He begins reading the message, his voice sounding agitated. "The Culmordis want us to bring them four Paedor families. In exchange for the prisoners, they promise not to continue their attacks on us."

Raelot, with his wide unnatural orange eyes, immediately steps forward with a raised drink. "The lying dirtbags. They'll never stop."

"Doesn't matter." Current scrunches the paper in his fist and tosses it to the floor. "We do what they want. It's for peace...even if it's momentary."

"You're only saying that for your girl's sake." Hywill gestures with his cigarette to where I sit. "She will end up dead the same as all the others you've brought here."

Dunn walks over to me and I feel his hand hovering above my shoulder. But he doesn't touch me. "It's a trick, Cure. You know that. We all know that."

"Dunn, you, Raelot, Hywill, and Wheelden find the rest of the boys. Do whatever you have to when rounding up families. Tell them they either come to the Brigehouse without a fight, or you all receive a worse fate on my order."

I stare straight ahead at Current as he watches them exit the Brigehouse one by one. Dunn takes the longest to leave, and I can feel the ends of his hair brushing against my face. He's leaning down to whisper something in my ear.

"Dunn!" Current snaps.

Dunn straightens, quickly moving away from me. He looks long at Current before passing him and grabs a gun on his way out the door. Current looks over his shoulder at me and then at Bramy sitting on the other side of the room. "You mind giving us a minute, brother?"

"No problem," Bramy says. He gathers up a stack of cigars and playing cards and heads toward the back room.

I know something bad is coming. Another disgusting act beyond comprehension. I don't leave my chair as Current circles from behind. He kisses my cheek, rubs his hands over mine, and forces me to stand. "Don't worry about Bramy, sweetlie. He's heard all this before."

I don't see any spiders or rats to keep me company. I can't reach an open window. I breathe out hard, bite back a sob, and wait for it to be over.

24

Dunn

"Why does Bramy get to stay behind?"

"Maybe because Current still feels guilty about forcing him to watch his brother's execution."

I walk behind Enbraet and Hywill, listening to their conversation. They're both sixteen and have the innocence of five-year-old children when they talk about anything.

"Current doesn't feel any guilt," I chime in.

"How do you know? Even if you hate his methods, Dunn, at least you can admit he's shown more mercy than the other gangs."

"None of us show mercy," I say. "There is no kind way to carry out an order like this."

"Well, I don't hate his methods," Hywill says. "I knew what I was signing up for."

"And that's why he gives you the biggest gun, Hywill." I slow my pace and stop to lean against an alley wall. "You two try your luck at luring the Ranhaas family out. I'll keep watch."

Hywill frowns as he notices my hesitation. "You gotta do some of the dirty work, Dunn. I'll tell Current if you don't."

"I do plenty for him. Get your ass in the house."

They glower as they leave me alone in the alley. I hold my breath, waiting to hear the scuffle and combative shouts. Fifteen minutes pass and it's still silent. *What are they doing? Did the family just surrender?*

"Parents weren't home but the girls were. Hey, Dunn! Walk the Ranhaas daughters back with us to the Brigehouse!"

Oh no. Those girls are only six and nine.

I step out from the alley, seeing Hywill and Enbraet each holding tight to the wrist of a girl.

Dammit.

"Does this count as one family?" Hywill asks.

"I bet we'll be the first ones back," Enbraet says excitedly.

I hate this. I look into the eyes of the six-year-old and she looks back at me. "They didn't fight back?"

"No. We told 'em they'll come home after a treasure hunt."

Dammit. Dammit. Dammit. I shake my head. But I follow behind. The six-year old glances over her shoulder and then submissively lowers her eyes to the ground. *She knows. What can they do against the Ravabrigs?*

What can I do against Current?

25

Riverduna

Current gives me a new piece of paper and a list of numbers to write down. He knows my need for a distraction. "Do you hear that, River?" he says.

I follow his gaze to the door.

"They're bringing the families. It's time to send a message back to the Culmordis." He walks around the table with his cigar, leaning close to my face. "You will write it and you will command my raven to deliver it."

I want to say no. I don't want to be a part of this cruel exchange. But I'm in the house of a gang. There is no negotiation.

"Tell them to expect their victims by nightfall. And sign it with me, sweetlie."

I lift my pen off the paper. "I'm not a Ravabrig," I say.

"Sign it. You help me lead this gang." He puts his arms around me, takes the pen, and signs his name. "You're one of us, Riverduna." He forces me to hold the pen again and guides me in signing my name. I hardly breathe.

"Now go out. Step outside and I'll bring Illdam to you."

I do as he says, picking up my skirt as I cross the doorway. The fog is swirling in and the wind is picking up. There is a mass of people outside the Brigehouse. All Paedors. All of the Ravabrigs are present. I can easily see which of the people are meant to be taken to the Culmordis; the victims look subdued after going through aggressive confrontations.

"Here," Current says. He sets Illdam on my wrist and lifts my arm up. "Tell him to take the message. Whistle."

Everyone is waiting for me to obey the command. I catch Dunn's eye in the crowd; he's staring directly at me. His shoulders raise as he takes a deep breath, and then I hear him exhale. He doesn't look like a fighter right now. He looks like a frightened little boy.

Loyalty to the Ravabrigs. Disloyalty to the Skies. I draw in a breath and blow out a low whistle. When I see Illdam spread his wings and fly east, I turn around, stare grimly up at Current's nod of approval, and go back into the Brigehouse.

26

Dunn

"Not gonna fill me in on the day?"

I look up from my spontaneous woodworking to see Tempest drinking a cup of tea. It's strange to see her without alcohol. "Just another terrible order that had to be carried out."

"I haven't seen you playing with a piece of wood since you were a boy."

"I'm not playing," I say, keeping my head down. "I'm making a whistle."

"What for?"

"I don't know yet. Just needed something to do since I'm skipping practice and the fights."

"Ah, I see. Mental frustration."

"Could you go upstairs, Tempest? I don't feel like talking. Bring Katy with you."

"Goodness. You really are upset."

"Please go," I say.

Five children sent to torturous deaths. Riverduna watching. Even if she is a Paedor like the rest of us, her eyes don't look like the other women's on the streets. It's like everything is a new horror to her. If Current doesn't give her one of his guns soon, I'm giving her one of mine.

27

Riverduna

"I saw you drinking wine with Dunn. Looks like you enjoyed that."
Current speaks as he undresses and throws his clothes on the floor.

I look toward the open window. *I could try to run.*

"Wanna drink with me?" he asks.

Amos comes in holding two bottles of wine. He tosses both to
Current and winks at me before backing out and closing the door.

Current can't keep me here forever. He knows I belong out there. I make
a run for the window, breathing rapidly when my fingers touch slate.
Yes.

"Bad move, River."

I'm halfway onto the roof when Current's hands are around my throat.
I try to kick back at him but only feel air. He slams me to the floor.

"Current," I sob. "Get off!"

Putting his whole weight on top of me, he gulps down one of the
wine bottles and smashes it right next to my head. Pieces of glass fly
in my eyes. I scream for him to let me up. But his fingers dig into my
neck and I can't breathe. *I can't breathe. He's gonna kill me. I won't run,
Current. I'll be good.* I see the snarl on his lips and stop pushing back. I
stop kicking. *I can't breathe. Dunn... help me...*

I can't turn my head as Current's choking me, but I look past his face at the ceiling. Four candles are burning in this room. The light is dim. Faint shadows around me. *I need air. I need to breathe.*

My view of Current is gone.

I see nothing but a starless black.

28

Dunn

Tempest is late. I walk around the house with Katlene, feeding her with her bottle and whispering the Echo Song. That song's been stuck in my head recently and I don't know why.

"Dunn? You there?"

I look back at the loud knocking. *Not Tempest.* It's her younger sister. "Come in, Harvest," I say.

Harvest bounds through the door, unnecessarily slamming it behind her. "Dunn, I'm sorry. I'm sorry I'm late."

"You're late for what? Where's Tempest?"

Out of breath, Harvest drops into the rocking chair and lights a cigarette. "She was poisoned. Told me to come watch the baby."

"Poisoned? When did that happen?"

"Last night. She spent the night with Anglaus and she and one other fell ill."

"But she's the most vigilant person I know, Harvest."

"I know." Harvest stares at the fire, kicking a stray ember away from her skirt. "But some of your Ravabrig boys showed up and demanded she join their drinking game. You know how she is. Never backs down from a challenge."

"They brought the alcohol, didn't they? Probably that bloody rum that they've been trying to get rid of in the Brigehouse."

"It was rum and wine. I watched some of the game and Tempest went to town on it. She let them pour it halfway through. I guess it's just her luck."

I bet they're watching the house. Listening to us talk. "Harvest, please do me a favor." I come close, holding out Katlene for her to take. "Watch Katlene for a few minutes."

"I can watch her all day, Dunn. I just can't be here at night."

I nod. *She's still looking for her daughters' killers.* "Avenge Cora and Bronta. I know."

"Tempest should recover within a week."

"Well, now I need someone here at night too. I don't feel as safe anymore." *Not with the way things are going in Dredgar.*

Harvest grins as she rocks faster in the chair. She sits Katlene up in her lap, keeping her from sliding down. "Hire Current's girl."

Sigh. Can no one in Anglaus keep their mouths shut? "I'll see what he allows me to do. Thank you for staying with my sister."

"You're like family to Tempest, Dunn. I'll do anything you need," she says.

I force a smile and go out the door. *The Brigehouse. This will get old.*

29

Riverduna

I eat spoonfuls of porridge as slowly as I can. I don't feel like leaving the house. Melnie seems to understand this and keeps my bowl filled.

"River, do you want me to show you some chores?"

"If it's fine with Current," I say.

"Of course it is." Current bends down to kiss my hair. "Take it easy today, sweetlie. I'll come back at noon and we can have you do more writing at the Brigehouse. Sound good?"

I nod. My eyes are still stinging from the bits of wine bottle glass. I feel like I have a fever.

"Look after her, Mother. Keep her busy."

Melnie smiles as she brings two cups of tea to the table. "Go, Current. We'll be good."

I don't fully relax until the door closes behind Current, and then I give a sigh so loud and long that Melnie immediately knows what's on my mind.

"At least the glass didn't blind you," she says. "But maybe try not to run next time."

"You speak as if it's normal. Does Amos throw things at you?"

Melnie looks around before sitting down and responding in a soft voice. "Depends how drunk he is. Not all Paedor men are this aggressive, but all Ravabrigs are."

I pick up the teacup, inhaling the spicy cinnamon smell. "But Dunn is a Ravabrig too, right? He doesn't act like the rest of them."

"You're right. He's got a softer heart despite his champion fighting." She takes a sip of tea. "Poor boy spent weeks hiding in the shadows after Current stabbed his eye out."

What? Aren't they friends? "Why would Current do that?"

"Amos and I only know Current's side of the story. Some sort of challenge between them dissolved into a screaming match and then the worst of insults. Sounds petty but it is what it is."

My stomach churns thinking of the fear and pain that Dunn went through when he was attacked by Current. *Why would anyone do that to their friend?* "How old were they when that happened?"

"Dunn was ten. That was the day…" Suddenly Melnie gets up and takes the dishes from the table. She stacks them in the corner kitchen without saying anything else.

"Melnie?" I stand up to follow her. "That day was what?"

"Dunn just… he accused Amos of something terrible."

"What did he say?"

"Nevermind, Riverduna. Can you help me start sweeping the rooms? The men track so much dirt in here."

I know I shouldn't ask so many questions. But they say I'm one of them now. Wouldn't I get the privilege of learning their secrets too? I glance down to see a rat run across the floor. There is filth and smoke and cobwebs in every corner of the house. Cleaning it sounds like a pointless endeavor.

"Here." She pushes the broom into my hands and returns to the dishes.

One with the family. Okay, I can handle this. I'm thankful to not be with Current right now.

30

Dunn

The Brigehouse has an unusually cheery atmosphere. Wheelden is sitting on the floor trying to fix a broken fiddle, Current and Raelot are poking fun at Bramy and his card tower, and Hywill and Enbraet are drunkenly singing a song that they clearly made up within the past ten minutes. None of them have blood on their clothes. *It's like yesterday's traumatic event never happened.*

"Where's Riverduna?" I ask. "You didn't drag her with you today?"

"My mother's letting her help with chores at home. I figured she could use some rest since I roughed her up last night."

I walk over to Wheelden who is holding a cigar up in the air. He grins and goes back to the fiddle when I take it.

"What did you do to her, Cure?"

Current shrugs and sips his whiskey. "The usual."

"What did you do when she fought back?"

He frowns. "How do you know she fought back?"

"All Paedor females fight back when they don't want it."

"Well, she tried to run from me. In the end she blacked out."

Raelot and Bramy trade amused glances.

"Don't know what's getting into her," Current says. "She didn't start that way."

Idiot. "You don't know how to be gentle with anyone, Current. What else is she supposed to do?"

"Can't say I'm not proud of River's feisty spirit. Few more nighttime romps with her and I'll give her a gun."

"Brutality isn't the way to convert a girl," Bramy says. "She's gotta learn the graceful part of it too. And you're such a beast, Current. Too much of a beast for her to train with."

"What do you suggest then?"

Bramy looks annoyed when Current leans over his tower. "Knock it over. Go ahead. Patience never was your skill."

A couple more of the boys enter the Brigehouse and I walk to the middle of the room. "Current," I say, pointing my cigar at him, "Tempest was poisoned. I need to borrow Riverduna for use as a nanny at night."

Current sits quietly for a moment. I can see him thinking through each word I said. He finally stands and comes to me, staring down at me in his menacing way. "What makes you think I'd just lend my girl out to you? And I don't give a bloody hell about your nanny falling ill."

I want to tell him about the Ravabrigs having a role in the poisoning, but the rational side of my mind takes over. "Look, it's just for a week. Maybe less if she comes back sooner."

"Your nanny only came in the day. Why do you need someone at the house at night if you're there with your sister?"

"Because the streets are getting worse. Yesterday... I couldn't imagine if I had been forced to give up Katlene. The Culmordis could've been specific with the victims they wanted. They could've asked for me and my sister and I know you would've allowed us to die by their hands."

Current is silent. The others are looking at us.

"Please, Current. You know I wear myself out in the fights. I'm not always alert in the middle of the night. It's worse now out there. You all know it."

His face changes from serious to a half-smile. But I see the dark intent in it. "Promise you'll get back into the pit fights soon. I know you wanted a break from it, but I hope you return to practicing. We need you to represent the Ravabrigs."

"I will. Just a bit more time for me to get my head together."

"And I expect you to bring Riverduna back to me in the morning. Promptly by seven."

"Yes." I do my best to hide my grin. "Seven to seven. Deal?"

He starts to stretch out his hand but falters. "And, Dunn, you will gift two of your mother's swords to me for each night that River works for you. My parents have admired that collection for years. A quality trade, don't you think?"

"Yes." I clasp his hand, nervous to fulfill his wishes yet also determined to provide protection for Katlene and Riverduna. *Should I fail either of them, I'll want to die.*

II

Part Two: The Paedor And The Sky

31

Riverduna

By the time I've finished sweeping the second floor, I notice that Melnie has stopped trailing behind. I guess she trusts me not to run.

"Hi, River."

I look to see Dunn in the hallway. "Where's Current?"

"Downstairs. He said I could come up to talk to you."

Talk about what?

"My sister's nanny fell ill and I'd like you to work in my house. It would be at night so I'd be home too."

His voice is gentle. Encouraging. But I don't believe it. *Why would Current let me go?* "I want to," I say. "But Current—"

"Don't worry about Current. We came to an agreement. You will be with me and Katlene from seven at night until seven in the morning. I'll walk you to and from my house."

I nod at him and he smiles.

"Am I going with you tonight?" I ask.

"Yes. Right after dinner."

No more terrible nights here. Yes. Thank you, Dunn.

* * *

I don't pay attention to anything at dinner other than Dunn's replies to Current's parents' questions. They like to agitate him with their words. But he always seems to know the right thing to say.

"When you getting back into the pit?" Amos asks.

"Soon. Maybe tomorrow or the night after."

"The Ravabrigs need you to maintain their honor," Melnie says. She gives a sympathetic gaze to Current and Current slyly grins at Dunn.

"There are others in the gang who can fight," Dunn says. He looks ready to throw his fork at Current's face.

"Not like you. You've taught yourself the perfect technique."

Dunn looks coldly at Amos. "Anyone can learn my skills. It's just survival."

"Survival indeed. We know you'll keep River safe," Current says. "Be sure to bring her back on time."

"I will." Dunn half-smiles as he looks at me. "I'll keep her out of trouble."

Trouble. As if I'm the one that needs to be told that.

32

Dunn

The walk to my house is calm. It's a relief as usual to get inside where it's safe and warm, but I notice Riverduna is uncomfortable.

"You good, River?"

"It still feels like Current's house," she whispers.

"The layout may be similar, but I promise that mine is different." I note the empty room and call up the stairs, "Harvest? You have Katy?"

"Yes!" she says back. She comes down with Katlene in her arms, looking nervously over her shoulder. "I had to run an intruder off."

I take Katlene from her, holding her tight against me. *This nightmare...* "When did they break in?"

"Don't worry, Dunn. I shot 'em out the third floor window. The asshole barely got inside the room before I sent him flying back out."

Way too much like her sister. "A Ravabrig?"

"No. Ferrelium. Stupid sword and all."

Ugh. The timing of this news couldn't be worse. I look at Riverduna, who's standing as close to me as she can without pressing against my side. But she's smiling at Harvest. I breathe out a sigh.

"You're the girl Anglaus has been talking about," Harvest says to Riverduna.

"I guess I am."

"I swear all the gossip is with good intention."

Sure it is. Anglaus and their secrets. "Harvest, I've a favor to ask," I say. "Would you mind lighting the lamps for me on your way back?"

"All right. One time I'll do your job." She points from me to Riverduna. "But tomorrow night you give her some time alone while you do that."

Riverduna is calmly walking around the house now, studying every little thing in the room.

"Fine. You'll be here again in the morning?"

"I will," Harvest says. She exits without a look back, and I hear her muttering to herself as she begins her nightly hunt on the streets. *Good luck on your vengeance. We all need it.*

* * *

An hour passes in complete silence. I remain downstairs holding Katlene while Riverduna explores each room. She stops at the second floor and turns around, picking up her skirt as she returns to the fire and sits in the rocking chair.

"Would you like to hold Katy?" I ask.

She nods.

"I'll have to teach you the Echo Song. It's the only song that stops her crying."

"Is it a lullaby?"

I smile, gently passing Katlene to her. "Not really. My mother made it up as a way to call me back home. I often stayed out past dark and would forget where our house was."

"So she would sing the Echo Song to you?"

"Yes. She sang a verse and then I sang one. Back and forth until we found each other."

"She sounds like a sweet mother," Riverduna says.

"Yeah." I sit on the floor and watch the fire crackle.

We both enjoy the quiet until Riverduna asks another question with her melodic voice.

"Dunn, what makes you a champion fighter?"

"I'm small like you, right?" I say. "It seems like I wouldn't win. But I keep myself balanced. I dodge right where I'm at. Moving fast only wastes energy so I try to save quick maneuvers for a blood-strike."

She rocks a litter faster when Katlene squirms in her arms. "What's that?"

"It's when either opponent is aiming to permanently wound the other."

"And how do you know that it's a blood-strike and not a normal strike?"

"It's in their eyes."

"Their eyes?"

I see the confusion on her face and shift to my knees, lining myself up with the rocking chair. I grip the sides of it and stare into her eyes, breathing softly as she stares back. "I never take my eye off of theirs."

33

Riverduna

Dunn has a mischievous look on his face as he goes on. "I can read a person's intention just by a three second look into their eyes. And then I visualize how I would take them down."

The way he's staring at me... gives me chills. But I can tell he's trying to respect my space.

"What do you see in my eyes, Dunn?" I ask.

He grins before answering. "I see a very, very long chase if I gave you the option of a head start."

"And what's my intent?"

"To love. To show empathy to those who deserve none." He sits back, poking a metal rod in the fire. "Intention is everything, darlie. Knowing a person's intent helps you understand how to fight and defend."

"Is fighting the same as defending?"

"No," he says. "Fighting takes nothing but blind rage. Defending comes from love."

I watch him get up and walk to the kitchen. He brings a bowl over and sits down with it. *What is that?*

"If someone came in right now," he says, "and tried to steal Katlene, I would attack them to defend her. And to defend you. There is no focus in fighting, but defending gives you tunnel vision. More lives are saved when it's done right." He holds the bowl out to me. "Hazelnuts?"

I'm reassured to see him eating one himself so I also take one and munch it. *So much calmer in this house. Doesn't feel real.*

"I'll let the fire die out, darlie. You can sleep in any room you want. Even here if you like."

"I don't want a bedroom," I say. "No beds. Just the floor."

"Okay. Want me to take Katy for a bit?"

I shake my head. "I got her."

He smiles. "I'm glad you're good with children. Good sign that she's asleep."

"But what about the Echo Song?" I ask. "Can you teach it to me?"

"Now?"

"Yeah."

He looks into the fading embers and I don't think I'll hear it, but eventually he starts humming, and then a line of gentle words comes from his mouth: "Aquila volans, auferet nox libertas, libertas. Aquila volans, aquila volans, libertas, libertas."

"What language is that?" I ask.

"Latin."

"What does it mean?"

Dunn lies down on the floor. "All I know is it had something to do with the night sky and constellations of stars. But the sad thing, darlie, is that I've never seen stars. I'm sure you haven't either."

I look down at sleeping Katlene's face and think about all the stars I've seen in Nameus. On the rare clear nights, I've seen the entire night sky open up and sparkle like magic. "No," I whisper. "I've not seen them."

You have no idea, Dunn. I want to tell you all about where I come from. I decide to remain in the rocking chair, hoping I can keep holding Katlene as I try to fall asleep. I don't know what time it is, but I know it's the best night I've had since following Current down to the streets.

No one's going to hurt me this night.

* * *

"River, wake up. We gotta go."

I open my eyes to find myself lying on the floor. There's a blanket over me. But I still have my clothes on.

"Riverduna, come. It's almost seven. Current will not react well to us being late."

I sit up and look to where Dunn is standing by the door. He's waving me over. The Anglaus woman from last night is in here again. She is holding Katlene. "Go, girl," she says to me. "You don't want to make Current angry."

"Okay." I get up and follow Dunn out the door, sensing how messy my hair is. I try to fix it into a seamless bun at the top of my head but it sags into a ponytail.

"How'd you sleep?" Dunn asks. He's walking fast - I quicken my pace to keep up with him.

"Better than I have. But how did I end up on the floor?"

"If you're thinking I moved you there, darlie, I promise I didn't. You were sleepwalking."

Sleepwalking? I've never done that. "What do you mean?"

"You did. Had a nightmare I think."

I look at the alleys on either side of us and up at the buildings. "Why are we walking to the Brigehouse?"

"How'd you know that's where we're going?"

"I've memorized the routes," I say.

"Well, one of the Ravabrig ravens brought me a message an hour ago. Current wants you to write out more codes."

More writing. That doesn't sound terrible. I hope Dunn pours some wine.

34

Dunn

"Bramy, where's Current?"

Looking up from cleaning his rifle, Bramy nods at me. "Where do you think? Business with the Ferrelium."

Business. That's too nice a word for what Current really does. "Someone else struck a bad nerve?

"I don't know. He seemed really upset when he came in."

"I'm surprised he's not here to make sure I brought Riverduna back safely."

Riverduna has already sat down at the table and begun writing. Bramy looks in her direction and then motions me to come in closer. "You two have fun last night?"

"I didn't do anything with her, Bramy."

"Damn." He sets his rifle against the wall and stands up. "Thought you would take that chance, man."

"No way. I'm nothing like Current." I take a cigarette from my pocket and light up, sitting across from Riverduna.

"That's quite an insult, Duncan."

Oh hell. Current's back.

"I swear, you two managed to be late and thought you would get away with it?"

"We made it on time, Current." I look at him as he crosses the room. He seems highly agitated. "Bramy can attest to that," I say.

"Regardless of timing," Current says, "I have a proposal for you, Dunn."

"What do you want now?"

"I want you to take on another fight tomorrow." He glances at Riverduna before looking back at me. "I spoke with Vilho. We changed the rules."

Vilho working with Current? I angrily blow out smoke. "Changed them when?"

"Last night. He and I talked over drinks."

"What's the change?"

"Weapons are now mandatory."

"But weapons have never been part of Cruftetin. The fight is between two men, with our fists. Nothing else."

"Well… I'd say the change is for the best. That's why I'm giving you time to practice." Current leans over and takes Riverduna's hand in his. "And now I get to spoil my girl, because I missed her so much last night."

I'm furious at Vilho. He's probably waiting for me at the pit. But I don't want to leave Riverduna. *If there was a way she could come with me…* "Hey, Current, what if River comes to watch me practice? I'll bring her to your house when I'm done."

"She stays," Current says. "You had her all night."

"But I could teach her the basics of swordplay."

"No." Current's completely focused on Riverduna, pulling her away from the table, toward the back room. "You make a kill in the pit, Dunn," he says without looking back at me, "and I'll let us both teach her a weapon."

I hear whimpering from Riverduna as Current forces himself on her.

This violence. This indignity. "Fight back, darlie," I whisper as I run out the door. "Fight that bastard." *Vilho, you son of a bitch.*

35

Riverduna

My body goes numb. I just stare at the blurred ceiling and patches of cobwebs. *If I'm calm it will end faster. If I'm calm. I'm calm...*

But then Current bites my neck. Hard. His fingernails scrape down my chest, piercing into my skin like a wolf. He's rough. Violent.

"Current," I breathe out. "Stop. Stop!"

He lifts his head, panting, dark eyes meeting mine. I groan at the throbbing pain and lash out, slapping him across the face.

"You ask for this, sweetlie," he growls.

"Stop!"

I curl my fingers against my palms, making fists, and when Current goes to bite my neck again, I swing for his eyes. He reels back and punches me.

I taste metal.

"You want to learn the hard way, don't you?"

No, no, no. I watch him get up and stand in the furthest corner of the small room. He motions for me to approach.

"Hit me back, Riverduna," he says. "C'mon."

I shake my head.

"Do it. Fight like a Ravabrig."

I look toward the locked door, hoping to see one of the boys come in to break up this nightmare. But none of them do.

"No one gets mercy," Current says. "You will be my tough Ravabrig wife."

"No." I sit against the wall with tears stinging my eyes.

Current runs forward and pins me down, kissing and biting me harder, not caring about the blood spilling from my nose and mouth.

Something inside me has snapped. Now I know what it's like to fight. I know what it's like to be violent.

36

Dunn

"Vilho!"

"Catch the sword, Dunn!"

I duck, stepping to the right. A two-handed sword comes flying toward me and lands in the dirt. Vilho laughs.

"Why are you throwing swords around?"

"It's a dull blade, don't worry."

I pick it up, cautiously eyeing Vilho as he grips his own sword and walks toward me.

"So," I say, "did I hear it right that you agreed to this new way of Cruftetin?"

"No one likes the old rules more than me, Dunn, but Current's reasoning was sound."

"What was the reasoning?"

He takes a swing at me, forcing me to run backward.

"Ravabrigs paid off several fighters outside of Dredgar to assassinate children if you don't start making kills."

Current's wicked game... "Clever ploy," I say.

Vilho and I circle each other as we maneuver our swords. "And he told me to tell you that Coald is the first child on the hit list."

Coald. Expendable little boy... he has no idea.

"Current and I were drinking when we talked so maybe I heard it wrong."

"You sound drunk now, Vil."

"Yeah. Gotta be," Vilho says with a grin. "He bribed me with a bottle of vodka."

"I haven't seen vodka in the streets."

"Well, someone smuggled it in. Tastes nice."

Ugh. Current. If he's threatened all the children in the streets, I know that means he's threatening Katy too. There is no choice but to face the pit again. Even if that means another encounter with Amos...

37

Riverduna

Bramy had wordlessly draped a blanket over my shoulders a couple hours after I returned to my writing. I'm shaking so badly that I can't write one proper number. The pain in my lower body is causing endless spasms. I lose track of time and energy, and by the time I see Dunn come back into the Brigehouse, I'm minutes from collapsing.

"River looks ill," he says to Current.

"She's definitely worn out. Want a cigar?"

"No. Close to seven, Cure. I'm taking her home."

"Sure." Current speaks calmly as he lights up. "Time flew today, didn't it? I didn't get much done except for making love with my little sparrow."

"You missed the chaos," Bramy says. "I swear they almost broke the door down this time."

I don't look at Dunn when he comes over to me.

"Hey," he says softly. "Come on."

I keep my head down and draw in a breath. *Walking hurts.*

"River." He drops to one knee and looks in my eyes. "You can hold onto me."

"I don't want to," I whisper.

He gestures for me to stand. "Lean on my arm."

The longer I remain here, the darker it will get outside. I push myself out of the chair and lay my hand on his forearm.

"Watch it, Dunn," Current says from his corner. He drunkenly laughs into his whiskey. "Don't beg for more trouble."

"I wouldn't dare cross a Ravabrig," Dunn says. Walking me out the door, he notices the pain on my face. "I'll have Harvest make you some lavender tea before she leaves, darlie. I need to light the lamps tonight."

* * *

Harvest already has a thick blanket laid out by the fire when we go inside. I sit down on it, feeling myself breathe deeper than I had for hours before.

"Can you make some tea for her, Harvest?"

"Yes. I'll stay until you get back."

"Thanks." Dunn glances at me once more before hurrying out the door.

The warmth is nice. But the chills don't stop.

"I'll get you another blanket," Harvest says. "You like lavender tea?"

"I'll drink it if you do," I say.

She sighs as she brings two cups over. "Fair. Current's done a lot of damage to your mental state."

"Thank you." I cradle the cup in my hands, waiting for Harvest to sit and drink hers.

"Of course." She looks back toward the kitchen. "Katlene's bassinet is over there. Was the quietest place for her to sleep three hours ago."

I breathe in the lavender. "I'm happy she has people to keep her safe."

"It's not that easy you know. With the way the gangs run each district, there isn't much of a chance of her surviving past ten years old. And you can bet that she'll be attacked if she ever steps out alone."

Harvest's hair is a dusty orange. Like a smoldering flame. All the Paedor women seem to have scattered strands of white or grey hair. *Everyone ages fast here.* "Current wants me to be his wife."

"You're going to have to figure out an escape then, aren't you?" Harvest says. She takes her empty cup back to the kitchen and picks up Katlene from her bassinet.

"Current's too strong, Harvest. Running makes it worse."

"Perhaps now that is true. But I know that one day there will be a new gang to replace the Ravabrigs."

I scoot closer to the fire, watching the sparks bounce around the logs. They look like fireflies.

"Anglaus," Harvest says. "We'll defend the people of Dredgar."

Women beating men in fights. I can't imagine such a thing. But then I think about Sashae. Her tough stance and how she talked to me at the pit. She could take on Current. *Maybe she would know how to set me free.*

38

Dunn

I don't know how to react when I come in the door. Riverduna is sitting under the kitchen table hugging her knees to her chest. She's quietly pushing one of Katlene's wind-up toys, a brass ladybug, on the floor. I look at Harvest for an answer but she just shrugs. She brings Katlene to me and whispers, "I think it's the thunder."

The downpour struck before I made it home, and I'm still wiping wet hair out of my eyes. The thunder could be louder, but I'm assuming it sounds like gunfire to Riverduna. *Why else would she be hiding under a table?*

"Darlie," I say to her when Harvest has gone, "would you like to see the rest of the house? I can show you where I make the mechanical toys."

"You made this?" Riverduna looks at the ladybug in her hand and then at me with wide eyes. "Where did the metal come from?"

"I have lots of it in my attic. That's where I tend to work on projects."

She starts to crawl out and yanks on her skirt when it gets caught in the floorboards.

"I want to see it," she says.

"Okay." I wait for her to start up the stairs and then I follow with

Katlene in my arms. "All the way up. Fourth floor."

The second we reach the top room, I hear Riverduna gasp, and I smile. Besides my parents and Tempest, she is the only other person to see my stockpile of metal and wood scraps. I know the rest of Dredgar would see it as junk. *But I'm proud of this.*

"Wow."

"Yeah," I say.

She touches the shelves and picks up each toy. Studies the pendants hanging on the walls. "I can't believe all of this can fit up here. This is a big attic."

I make a pile of blankets and set Katlene down on it. She happily plays with a knitted butterfly that Tempest had crafted in a haphazard fashion.

"Do you know what brings me peace, darlie? Making these metal beetles and ladybugs."

"I didn't think Paedors felt peace," Riverduna says.

"If I didn't seek peace, River, I'd be long dead. So would my sister. I fight for her and I build for her. If I don't calm myself, I'll destroy everyone who crosses my path. Anger is the most volatile of weapons… and I want to protect you from it."

She turns, toying with a beetle pendant. "Was Dredgar ever a peaceful place?"

"I'm not sure." I sit at my work table and pick up the wooden whistle I had made. The letters R and D are carved into it. *Never finished a project so fast.* "From what I learned as a boy, it's been seventy years give or take of this lawless, anarchist state. I wish it would change, but common people can't seem to alter the structure of society. I've been trying to figure out who is at the core of the violence."

"Any idea who?"

"Not one idea that can successfully take me to Brigandre. The tower to the north of us. I want to see who lives in it. Maybe evidence that has been left. Anything to see who the real mastermind or leader is."

"And you've tried to get there?" Riverduna asks.

"Many times. Every airship I've started to build, every bicycle or horse I've acquired has been taken from me and savagely destroyed."

"Well…" She walks around the room, fiddling with the pins in her hair. Then she faces the tiny window and says, "Have you traveled to Nameus? It would be easier to reach the tower that way."

"No. I've never been up there."

39

Riverduna

"I'm from there," I say.

"You're from Nameus?"

"Yes."

Dunn gapes at me. "Whoa. I knew there was something different about you. But I thought that you might just be a timid Paedor."

"Current led me down from the rooftops. He said he would keep me safe."

Shaking his head, Dunn leans forward and says in the lowest whisper, "Riverduna, you're one courageous Sky."

"I miss Nameus," I say. "I just want to go back. We can go together."

"But the danger won't end for you," he says. "It won't end for any of us."

"Let me guide you to the tower. The high ground is the safest road."

Dunn looks anxious, drumming his fingers on the table. "I'm afraid of heights, darlie."

"But don't you have to use a ladder to light lamps? That's high up too."

"That's nothing compared to the rooftops. And even if I could go to Nameus, there's no way to prevent the gangs from attacking us in our journey."

"Please, Dunn." I can't talk without pacing. I just want to go home. "I know every inch of it."

"Riverduna," he says. He stands and walks to me, gently placing a hand on my shoulder. "I'll think on this, okay? I know you want to be rid of Current. But we have to be careful or we will all pay the price."

"I know," I say. *The fog. My plushies. My books.* I think about the photograph I had tucked in my trouser pocket, wondering if it's still there. I reach under my skirt while Dunn looks at me like I'm crazy, and I pull the stained and torn photograph out.

"What is that?" Dunn asks.

I hold it up between two fingers, looking at it and then at him. "It's a photograph." *Half of one.*

"What do the words say?"

I glance at the back and see part of a message written in cursive: "Happy wedding, Amber & Darek. 2012."

"Twenty twelve," Dunn whispers.

"Yeah. I find these everywhere in Nameus." *From a different time. A different world.*

"These people look happy." He takes it from me and stares at the man and woman. "Where did they come from, River?"

"I don't know. But I know I belong up there."

Dunn hands the photograph back. "Brigandre may hold answers for me," he says. "But I still don't know if it's a journey worth taking." I hear a slight tremor in his voice when he adds, "Not if we have to endanger Katlene too."

We both look to where Katlene is babbling in the pile of blankets. *No.* I couldn't risk her falling victim to Current too. That's the last thing I want. But I have to get back to Nameus. *There has to be a way.*

40

Dunn

Both of us are trying to avoid discussing Nameus or Brigandre over breakfast. I know it's hard for Riverduna not to bring it up after telling me who she really is, but she knows, as well as I, the danger of speaking openly about it.

"Who do you think will be at the Brigehouse this morning?" she asks.

I set a bowl of porridge in front of her and sit at the table. "Bramy almost always is."

"He's been really nice to me."

"Yeah." I take a bite and realize it's burnt again. "He came from a close family."

"Do none of the other Ravabrigs live with their parents?"

"Most don't." I see Riverduna eating her porridge without hesitation. *Starving girl.* "Current does because his father is part of the gang."

"And what about Anglaus?"

I spit into the bowl. "What about them?"

"What side are they on?"

"No side, darlie. They do a lot more talking than fighting."

"You get annoyed by the talking, don't you?"

"Words don't accomplish much," I say.

"What if Anglaus took over the streets? They could make it safer."

I look at the sparkle in her eyes. *Anglaus is getting to her.* "Overrule the Ravabrigs? Not in my lifetime."

She stares at me for a minute before finishing her porridge. *Pretty girl with a wild mind.* I've heard how clever Skies can be.

* * *

The only person sitting in the Brigehouse is a little boy. *Coald.*

"Hey bud, what are you doing here?"

"Bramy said I could play with marbles."

I throw my coat over a chair and walk past his line of marbles on the floor. Riverduna goes to the table to write.

"Since when do you hang out in the Brigehouse?" I ask Coald.

"They told me to keep watch while they went out to practice."

"Practice?"

"Yeah, Dunn. Shooting."

I look around the room, surprised to see it empty. No guns, knives, or coats hung anywhere. *Why is it so immaculate?*

"Well, I'm going to pick a sword for my fight tonight," I say. "Any suggestions, Coald?"

"Yeah." He points up at a massive machete hanging on the wall. The only blade in the entire room. "That one."

"Are you serious?"

"Why not?" Coald gets up and walks over, doing his best to reach it for me.

"Hey, hey. I got it," I say. "Does Current want me to use this one?"

"He picked it for you, Dunn. Said it's for a gory kill."

Gory kill. Hearing Coald say those words so casually makes me cringe. "Killing is a last resort," I say. "Always."

"But Current said you have to kill. Kill to win. Or the other man will kill you first."

I look over at Riverduna who's listening to the conversation. Her attention is fully on Coald. She probably can't believe what's coming out of his mouth.

"Bud," I say, "can you get a wine bottle from the back room? I want to have a drink with River."

He grins. "Okay, Dunn." And he dashes away.

Riverduna looks past me when I come over to the table. "Does he fight too?" she asks.

"The Ravabrigs are training him to be heartless," I say. "But luckily, Coald's got some good left in him. Thing is... I don't know how much longer I can keep him alive out here." I resist touching one of Riverduna's stray curls, but I can't help from gazing into her eyes. *Just protect them. Protect her.*

"Are you going to kill your opponent tonight, Dunn?" she asks.

"I don't know. I'd rather you not be there to watch."

"I want to." She stands, looking like she wants to embrace me, but then walks over to the wall with the machete. "Can you show me how to hold it?"

Current won't like it if he sees me give her a weapon. But I've been wanting to see Riverduna wield a blade since the day I saw her pinned beneath the Ferrelium.

"All right." I take it off the wall just as Coald returns with the wine bottle. "Set it on the table, bud," I tell him.

"How do I stand?" Riverduna asks.

"Straighten your shoulders. Keep your feet and legs firm on the ground. I'm guessing you don't normally wear a skirt, do you?"

"No."

I smile. For a Sky she has blended in well as far as clothing goes. "You got it?"

"Yes."

She grips the machete, but I feel her shaking when I run my fingers down her arms.

"I'm just guiding you," I whisper. "I'm not going to hurt you."

"Okay." Her voice quivers. "Are all swords this heavy, Dunn?"

"This is closer to a knife than a sword. And you haven't handled a shotgun blade yet, darlie. Those are a different sort of beast."

"Shotgun blade," she repeats. "What's that?"

"I'll show you later. We better put this down before Current comes in."

She gives it back to me, and I see her breathing heavily. But she has a small smile on her face. *We're near the same height. Compact stature. It's sort of perfect.* I hang onto the machete as I go to pour us wine. Coald's back to sitting on the floor, flicking marbles around.

"I wish I could bring a sword into the bedroom," Riverduna says. "Leverage against Current."

"I know. We'll get you out of this, darlie." I keep it quiet that my thoughts are heavy on Brigandre. I want to get the journey over with. *Nameus is the last and best shortcut to the north.*

41

Riverduna

"Dunn! Dunn, Vilho wants you at the pit now!"

I look up to see Bramy running through the doorway. He goes straight to Dunn. "The fight's been moved up."

"Where have you been?" Dunn asks. "Where are the other boys?"

"Forget that. You need to go now. I'll walk Riverduna and Coald over."

Dunn gestures for me to quickly drink my wine after he takes a sip of his. "Did Current pay you to be his servant today, Bramy?"

"No. He's just busy getting drunk. We all are."

"Right. Bastard won't let me relax for an hour." Dunn slams his glass on the table and heads out. "Don't let River get lost in the crowd."

"I won't!" Bramy calls out. "Promise." He looks at me, waving for me to follow him. "C'mon, little sparrow. We gotta get front row seats to this."

"But what's the rush?" I ask. "Why does he have to fight now?"

"It's Current's call. The man's eager to see a bloodbath."

Bloodbath. I shudder when I walk beside him and Coald. I'm shocked at how many people are in the streets. Everyone is going in the same direction. To the pit.

"All these Paedors are smart," Bramy says with a grin. "They know it's a duel to the death. Best action we've had for weeks."

"Dunn's gonna lose his other eye!" Coald shouts excitedly.

"You think?" Bramy looks down at him, giving him a light pat on the head. "I think he's gonna come out in one piece. Maybe some minor wounds."

I hear chattering on all sides of me, horrified at how men and women are discussing the way Dunn's about to be killed. They laugh as they talk. *It's their game. Their fun.* "He has to win," I say. "He has to."

On our final steps to the pit, I catch sight of Current. My vision tunnels. I can taste vomit. *Please, no.*

"Bramy, you made it back! And you've brought my girl!"

I let him pull me in for an embrace, but he doesn't sound normal. His voice is raspier, words slurring. He smells like alcohol. His eyes are bloodshot.

"Yeah, we wouldn't miss this fight, Cure," Bramy says. "You know that."

Current throws a cigar to Bramy and returns his attention to me, bending down to force me into a long kiss. "If Dunn is killed, sweetlie," he says when he leans away, "you won't be the only girl in my house. I'll bring Katlene home too."

I take in small breaths, trying not to let my legs give out. *I'm panicking. Outright panicking.*

"You can be sisters," he says.

Stop kissing me. Get away.

"We really need to have a wedding already, don't we?"

I push against him as he tries to drag me into a less populated corner. *Not now. Please, stop. Stop.*

"Current!" a voice snaps.

Current whips his head around as I squeeze my eyes shut, fists clenched.

"Do that later, would ya? Taking all the attention from the champ again, you bastard!"

I don't know who has the guts to break Current away from me, but I'm left to stand alone, and I make my way as close as I can to the pit's edge, seeing Sashae from Anglaus across the way. The energy out here is intense. Everyone has fallen silent, waiting for Dunn.

But I see the opponent preparing to go down into the pit. And this man's holding two short swords. They look smaller than the one that Dunn helped me hold in the Brigehouse, but I can tell that there's something else attached to them. Shimmering black spikes.

42

Dunn

"I don't want to be a murderer, Vil."

"You're doing this for the children. Tell yourself that."

I slump against the wall in Vilho's tool shed, cigarette in hand. "It doesn't make me any better than Current or Amos. I want to be more than what they turned me into."

"Then you use this kill as a bargaining chip. Do what Current wants you to do and he will let you go to Brigandre." Vilho sits next to me. He pulls a bottle of rum out from beneath a pile of shovels. "He will see you as a loyal Ravabrig and reward you in whatever way you ask."

"He will have a new demand the second I mention Brigandre again," I say. "I'll be forced into making a new deal."

"Then take it and do what you have to do. Bloody hell, Dunn. If you don't go see the evidence for yourself, you'll be gabbing about this to me for the next ten years."

I crush the cigarette between my fingers and get to my feet. I pick up the machete.

"No more stalling," Vilho says. "No more playing nice. Kill, Dunn. Be proud of it."

But that's impossible.

* * *

I only need to take twelve steps to reach the edge of the pit. The crowd is deafening. Random objects are being thrown right and left. Dirt and sweat mixing in the air. The slight hint of sunlight through the haze would be pleasurable on any other day, but its warmth turns my stomach.

"Dunn, one hit! One hit!"

"Take his head off!"

"You got this, boy. Bring him down!"

The cheers unnerve me. I take several deep breaths before climbing down into the pit, and I know, without looking up, that Riverduna is standing at the edge.

"Charge him, Dunn!"

"C'mon! Kill him!"

The drunken screams of the Ravabrigs echo above me.

Instinct. It's all instinct. A mental game.

"How about we make this a long fight, Ravabrig?" My opponent is wielding dual blades with a wild snarl on his face. "Fill this place with blood."

Fighting is instinct. I duck as he comes at me.

"Swing! Cut his eyes out, Dunn!"

My back hits the opposite wall of the pit. I lose my breath and don't react quick enough to the next attack. Blood is dripping off his blades.

"Dunn!"

I feel the cuts on my forearms. Cuts on my legs. But this fighter isn't slicing to the bone. He wants to kill me slowly.

"Dunn, c'mon! Get him back!"

Vilho.

"Duncan, run that knife through his throat! Kill him!"

Current.

"I think you wanna die," my opponent says. He twirls his blades and charges forward, sending me to the dirt, stabbing harder into my arm. I feel the machete start to slip out of my hand and I grip it tighter.

"I'm not leaving my girls," I say to him. "Katy. River."

He looks at me like I've lost my mind.

"Son of a bitch," I breathe out. "I defend them!"

Bleeding from multiple stab wounds, knowing the pain will get worse when I clean them, I release an angry scream as I shove him off and drive the machete into his throat.

Survival.

Instinct.

43

Riverduna

I watch Dunn ascend out of the pit. His hair, his face, his entire body is soaked in blood.

"Dunn…" I whisper.

He looks at me and starts to say something, but Bramy and Current immediately run in and hoist him up in a celebration above the crowd. I don't see him smiling. I don't see him relieved. He just looks exhausted.

"Cruftetin champ!" Vilho yells. "Yes!"

Coald is jumping up and down next to me calling out Dunn's name. *Death is no victory.* Dunn tells the Ravabrigs to put him down and he limps toward me. Wordlessly, he grabs my hand and leads me away from the crowd, stopping when we reach an alley on the other side of the street.

"Riverduna," he says breathlessly, "I'm taking you back home. I'll talk to Current when he's sobered up tomorrow and we'll go to Nameus."

"Really?"

"Yes." He touches a hand to my cheek, looking me right in the eyes. "He will listen to me."

"I'll show you the way to Brigandre," I say.

"Yes." He suddenly grows solemn, brushing hair back from my face.

"I'm so sorry, darlie. I'm sorry for what you saw."

"But you survived." I look past the blood and dirt and let Dunn wrap his arms around me. I still feel scared out on the streets, but I feel safe when I'm with him. "You survived the fight."

44

Dunn

I learn that Current blacked out from drinking too much, and once we get home, I'm relieved to be able to rest without a looming threat.

"Dunn, I just bandaged you up. Stop pacing."

"Relax," I say to Harvest. "I need to gather the swords I promised Current."

"From your mother's collection."

"Yeah."

"That's all on the second floor. You shouldn't go upstairs yet."

"C'mon, Harvest. I'm all right."

"Well, you be sure he doesn't overexert himself until tomorrow," Harvest says to Riverduna.

"I'll get the swords for him," Riverduna says.

"Good. I'm heading out then."

I sit down in the rocking chair and wait for Harvest to exit before asking, "Darlie, do you want to hold a shotgun blade?"

Riverduna looks surprised but she nods.

"Look there on the rack behind you. Behind the top cupboard."

She turns around and goes to where I'm pointing.

"Lift it with both hands and bring it over to me."

With a grunt, she takes it off the rack. "Why is it called a shotgun blade?"

"Because it's two weapons in one. This is a sword built at the front of it. Different types of damage."

She studies each part of the shotgun, unsure of how to grip it.

"Here." I stand and hold it with her, moving her fingers to the proper placement. "This is how you prop it against your shoulder. Up a little further. Yeah. Like that."

Riverduna does everything I tell her to do. I sense her nervousness when her finger brushes the trigger.

"Relax. You don't have to ever use a gun if you don't want to. This is just a last resort."

"I want to learn," she says. "I want to protect myself."

"Guns aren't always the answer, darlie. Sometimes it just takes our own mental strength."

She lowers the shotgun with a loud exhale and hands it to me. "I'd rather fight with something lighter. A sword."

"Then go on up and bring some down. The sword collection is in the first room to the right."

I watch her go upstairs, and she returns minutes later with several swords from Mama's collection.

"What's this one called?"

"A cutlass," I say. I smile at her curiosity while placing the shotgun back on the rack.

"And these?" she says, holding up a set of tarnished blades.

"Hook swords."

Riverduna's excitement over the weapons helps me ignore my pain, and I can't help but pick out my favorite weapon and whip it around. *She makes me feel like a boy again. Such an endearing, playful spirit.* "And this is what we call a spike dagger. It's a weapon for thin, nimble fingers. Sharp at both ends, and spikes through its grip. You line up your fingers with the middle spikes as you hold it, careful not to cut yourself on them. Then you can wield it while running."

Her eyes light up when I give her a turn to hold it. "It's not heavy at all. I could use this on the rooftops."

"It is lighter than the others, but you must be cautious with it as you have no skill in blade fights."

"It can be learned though."

"Yes. My mother was a champion of swords. Anglaus gave this one to her for protection in the streets. Wielding it, slashing it overhead when the attackers are mobbing you… it's an elegant dance when done properly."

Riverduna lays the swords on the table and sits by the fire, reaching out to play with Katlene, who's on her little blanket.

"What was your mother's name, Dunn?"

"Imber," I say. "Latin for rainstorm."

"That's beautiful."

"Yeah. Her face was beautiful too until Father scarred it."

Riverduna looks up at me as I bring her a cup of lavender tea. "Your father hurt her?"

"Often. Mostly while she was pregnant with Katlene." I close my eyes at the thought of those months. I thought I was going to lose Mama back then.

"And what happened to her?" Riverduna asks me.

I turn away, unwilling to answer. She should know the answer by now. *Dead.*

45

Riverduna

I wake up to a bowl of porridge in front of my face.

"Morning, River."

Dunn seems well-rested as he moves around the room, gathering various supplies and putting them in a travel pack. "I'm meeting with Current after I take you to his house."

"What?" I push the porridge away and sit up, curls falling in my eyes. "Why do I have to go back there?"

"He sent us a message, darlie. He wants to speak with me alone and you are supposed to spend the morning with his parents."

"But I'm coming with you."

"Not yet. We have to do this the right way. If we make Current suspicious, neither of us will get out."

One more day. One more day of torture.

"Okay, Dunn," I say. "I'll wait there for you to come get me."

"Good. Just do what they ask of you and we'll be fine."

I'm going home. I'm almost home.

* * *

My stomach flips as soon as I enter Current's house. Melnie and Amos smile at me from the kitchen table, and Amos lifts a glass of whiskey. "River," he says, "go wait in the bedroom for Current. He would love it if you fixed your hair and put on some makeup."

I don't argue. Nor do I return his smile. I hold my skirt with one hand and go upstairs, my heart pounding the whole way. Fighting Amos is impossible. He's hurt me just as much as Current has. I fear him the same way.

When I get into the bedroom and look around, I notice changes. Awful changes.

I can't get out.

The windows are bolted down.

The door is locked behind me.

The mirror. The bed. I'm overcome with emotion and nausea when I look at the bed. I dry heave several times, almost collapsing. And then I sit in a chair and pick up a tube of lipstick, applying it like Amos told me to.

I can't do this.

My hand shakes as I set it down, and I pick up a comb to try to untangle the knots in my hair. I try to start braiding it.

This is not me. This is not Riverduna.

"No," I whisper.

I stare at my reflection in the mirror. I can't stand what I'm looking at. The loathing I have for this room and this family.

I punch the mirror once. I kick it. I punch again. Glass cuts across my fingers. But I keep punching. I see myself splintered in the fragments of glass. *A stranger. A bartering tool. All that's left.* I no longer see a Sky. I see an angry Paedor. And I've never felt anger like this. But I can't let them hear me.

I fall headfirst into the pillows and scream.

46

Dunn

Before I say a word to Current, he's handing me a cigar and lighting up his own.

"I figured you had something important to tell me," he says. "That's why I chose the alley instead of sitting among the boys."

"That's good," I say.

I try to hide my anxiety and enjoy a moment of silence with a cigar. But I can't stop from pacing the alley. I have to move.

"I thought you were done with Brigandre, Dunn."

I exhale quickly, turning to face Current. "How long have you known?"

"Your little obsession is no secret," he says. "And I realize that you won't be content until you satisfy your curiosity."

"I need Riverduna to lead me across Nameus, Current. It's the last route left."

"You do know that is a dangerous request."

"I do. But I did what you wanted."

Current grins, leaning against the wall. "You certainly did. That was a fine kill."

I'm a killer. He's proud that I'm a killer. I puff on my cigar, hoping for further reassurance from him.

"It should take no more than half a day for you to reach the northern district, Dunn. Fifteen miles from here to there."

I hold my breath. *What's the catch? What's the deal going to be?*

"Do not lag. Do not lose track of time."

"I won't," I say.

Current walks past me, eyes on the ground. He's actively thinking it through.

"I'll give you the night to situate yourselves on the rooftops. But you make your way to Brigandre as soon as it's light."

"Yes."

"When you get there, wait for me."

"But I'll bring her back. You can trust that I'll bring her back, Current."

"No." He shoves me against the wall, pressing his arm into my neck. "You wait there and I will come to you. Riverduna will be branded a Ravabrig and you will hold her down when I do it."

Branded a killer. A Ravabrig wife. She'll be his slave until she dies. "Current, she's not cut out for violence."

"River will be my wife whether she wants to or not. Just help me, Dunn. Help me brand her or we will do it to Katlene." He shoves me again, snarling into my face. "You've proven your loyalty. Don't mess it up."

"All right." I nod, bringing my hands up to push him away. "All right, Current. I'll do it your way."

Poker face. Hold the poker face.

"That's the old Dunn," he says with a grin. "I like that Dunn better."

Another plan, Dunn. Think. Protect Riverduna.

47

Riverduna

"Well, well, little sparrow, you've been busy in here."

I struggle to draw a breath as Current backs me into a corner.

"Barely gone for an hour and you've turned our room upside down. What's wrong, sweetlie? Desperate for my affection?"

No. How do you not see that I hate you? I hate this. How do you not see my pain? I duck when he tries to touch my face, circling to the other side of the room.

"I had a nice talk with Dunn," Current says. "We came to an agreement."

And?

"You will lead him from Nameus to the tower. And if Dunn returns without you, sweetlie, I will send every member of every gang to track you down."

Make him happy. Make him believe you are on his side. "When I come back, we can be married," I say.

"Yes."

I stand firm as he comes closer. "I'll stay in this room as long as you want me to."

"Promise?"

"I promise, Cur-"

He kisses me hard, pushing me down on the bed. But I don't fight him. I just take it.

It's almost over. I hold in a sob. *I'm almost home.*

48

Dunn

"Just keep looking up, Dunn. Don't stop climbing."

I'm tempted to go against my rational judgment and look down as I climb after Riverduna, but I decide not to. I've got Katlene strapped to my back as well as my pack of necessary survival items, and I don't want to think about the fact that I am several stories above Dredgar.

"You okay?" Riverduna calls.

"Yeah. I'm fine. A little dizzy, but fine."

"Isn't Brigandre going to be even higher? I've heard people say it's twenty stories at least."

I blow out a hard breath as I grip the slate and pull myself up. "I'm not going to find what I need in sky high rooms. I'm sure all the evidence will be at ground level."

"How do you know?"

"I just have a feeling," I say.

Riverduna is standing taller now that we are above the streets. *Beautiful Sky.* It's intensely cold and the fog is thicker than anything I've seen on the ground. The wind cuts through bone.

"This is brutal, River," I say.

"But it feels so good!"

I watch her run in one direction and then she comes back, taking a giant leap from one section of slate to another. She is happy and relaxed for the first time since I've met her. *After what Current put her through...*

"Thank you, Dunn," she says. She lies down, staring up at the night sky with a childish grin on her face.

I notice bright stars shining through a gap in the fog. "Wow."

"Nameus knew I was coming home," Riverduna says. "Brought out the stars for us."

I set my pack down and position Katlene against my chest to keep her warm. I walk around to get used to the open space of the rooftops.

Magic. The shimmering stars seem to reflect like flecks of gold in Riverduna's brown eyes.

"Darlie," I say softly, "you're a star brought to Earth."

She smiles. "So is Katlene."

"Then what am I?" I ask.

Without hesitation she says, "You're a meteorite."

And we burst into laughter.

This is the first time I've heard her laugh.

* * *

After an hour of trying to settle down and fall asleep, Katlene starts to cry, and Riverduna gladly takes her from me and bounces with her while quietly singing the Echo Song. I find myself closing my eyes to her sweet voice, and despite the thrashing wind, I feel content on the rooftops.

"River? What happened to your parents?"

"I found them dead."

"Where?"

"It was in an attic we would visit as a family. Brothers too."

I prop myself up against the remnants of a chimney. The stones dig into my back. "Do you know how they died?"

"Well, a fellow Sky said it was a lightning strike."

A lightning strike? "And you believed that, darlie?" I ask.

Riverduna paces back and sits down next to me. Katlene is half-asleep in her arms. "Why shouldn't I?"

"I've heard that Skies can be very trusting, but being so close to a violent world, I'd think it was murder."

She takes a hazelnut when I offer her one. "I never thought I had to be fearful in order to live."

"Fear is survival. That's what I was taught."

"Did your parents teach you that?"

"The streets taught me that, darlie."

"Then what happened to your parents?" Riverduna sounds concerned now. "Are they dead too?"

I look down, crushing the last cigarette in my fingers. *No more. Chew gum, Dunn. Find another crutch.* "Been dead for two and a half months," I say. "Killed."

"But... that's so recent." She looks at sleeping Katlene. "She's so little."

"I know. I've done what I can to make sure she survives." I unwrap a piece of gum and put it in my mouth. *Not the same.* "I fight in the pit to feel better. It distracts me from the loss."

Riverduna nods. She scoots closer, leaning against the chimney too.

"And I also fight for another reason," I say.

"What is that?"

If she only knew the comfort she brings me... The last words I want to tell her. "To forget what Amos did to me."

"Current's father."

"Yes."

"What did he do?"

I look her directly in the eyes. Our faces are just inches apart. "The same thing that Current has done to you. I was nine when it started. It went on until I was thirteen."

Riverduna lifts a hand to her mouth. She shakes her head. "I'm sorry."

Yeah. I sigh as I look out at the night, wishing I had something big and fragile to throw. "I wish it was Amos in that pit. I wish it was him and Current every time I hit someone."

"I'm sorry, Dunn." She touches my arm. "I'm sorry he hurt you."

"You have the same pain, darlie." I bite down on my lip when my voice breaks. "I'm sorry too."

49

Riverduna

The middle of the night on the rooftops proves to be too cold for Dunn and Katlene, so I lead them into an attic.

"This house is abandoned," I say.

"How can you tell?"

"The door to the lower floors is sealed. We don't have to be as quiet up here."

I kneel down and sift through a stack of dusty books, finding a plush giraffe among them. I clutch it to my chest and turn around. Dunn's watching me, head tilted. He looks confused.

"Where's that toy from?"

"I find them all over. And look at this." I take him to a wall and point at the rows of photographs.

"Why are they blurry?" he asks.

"I don't know. But look at how happy the people are. And the families. Look at the puppy in this one."

I touch each photograph and Dunn smiles as he studies them with me. We talk about the people in them and one by one create our own stories of what happened in the photographs.

Finally feeling sleepy, I start to lie down, and Dunn holds a small object out to me. "I want you to have this, River."

"What's that?"

"A wooden whistle."

I take it and inspect it while settling under my blanket. "Why are you giving me this, Dunn?"

"I made it for you. If we somehow get separated along the way, for any reason, I want you to blow it, and I'll know to come for you. The sound is unique."

I put it to my lips and before I can breathe out, Dunn lays his hand over the top of mine. "Not now. It'll wake Katlene and anyone else within a mile's range. But you can wear it around your neck. So you don't lose it."

"Okay." I clutch it close and I roll to my side. "Thanks, Dunn."

"You're welcome," he says. "Goodnight, Riverduna."

Night, Dunn.

50

Dunn

Too many voices. Loud voices. I jolt awake. "What in bloody hell?"

"It's okay, Dunn. They're Skies."

Riverduna is standing there with a man and a woman who look to be in their thirties. *Skies indeed.* They're all dressed in thin cotton shirts and trousers, including Riverduna, who appears to have changed outfits while I was asleep.

"I didn't think you had friends in Nameus," I say.

"I just met them, Dunn. They wandered into the attic."

"Wandered?" I make sure Katlene is nearby before shaking the dust out of my hair and getting up. "Don't Skies know when an attic is occupied?"

"Oh, he's definitely a Paedor," the woman says.

"A keen insult," the man says with a nod.

Riverduna steps between them and me, arms out in defense. "Dunn's my friend. He saved me."

"River, we may have just met, but clearly you haven't much experience in the world. No Paedor can be trusted."

I frown. *What is this Sky's deal?* "I promise that I'm different."

"How old are you?" the man asks, crossing his arms.

"Early twenties. You don't need to know specifics."

"And you, Riverduna?"

"Seventeen," she says.

Distractions. That's all these Skies are. It's almost like the Ravabrigs planted them here as a way to slow us down. "We have to get going," I say. "We've got thirteen miles ahead of us at this point I imagine."

"And where are you going with her?" the woman asks.

"Brigandre," Riverduna answers for me. "He's looking for something important there."

"Yes. And we don't have much time." I go to pick Katlene up but Riverduna beats me to it, clutching her close.

"And do you have a plan for crossing the minefield?" the man asks.

Riverduna and I look at each other. "The what?"

51

Riverduna

"You need a guide to get across it. Almost no one survives the journey there and back."

I see the worry and frustration in Dunn's face as he listens to the male Sky. But I know that Skies have wisdom. I may not have traveled as far as some, but as a whole, our culture is very observant to the dangers of the outside.

"How big is the field?" Dunn asks.

"Five miles."

"And what is the danger?"

"Explosives buried underground. One wrong step leads to mutilation at least. Or death."

"I'll trust them to lead us, darlie, if you do."

"I do trust them," I say. "We have to get across."

He nods and heads out of the attic. I take a moment to be sure of my decision, looking long and hard at my new acquaintances. "You didn't tell me your names," I say.

"Autana and Skyntar," the woman says. "We're fraternal twins. And we like to say that we're the watchers of the north."

"Do you sleep in attics like me?"

"Sometimes. We prefer to stay on the move."

I step out with them and we follow Dunn. I notice him slowing down to listen to our conversation.

"Few Skies are as young as you are, Riverduna," Skyntar says. He hops over a gap in the slate. "Most of us are beyond twenty-five."

"What happened to the children?"

"Lots of killings. We never learn the name or face of who does it, but we know it's one of the Paedors. Always a Paedor."

"That's enough!"

Dunn runs back, spitting angrily in Skyntar's face. "I am not a killer. I defend."

"Your behavior toward us says otherwise."

"I wouldn't hurt an innocent person. Not all Paedors are bad, Skyntar. And not all Skies are good."

Autana sighs loudly as she moves into the front. "The longer you live, the more you learn. And the more you learn who not to trust."

"River." Dunn grabs my arm and leans in to whisper in my ear. "Skies or not, don't take them at their word. This is our journey. Not theirs."

I sense his heightened fear as we move further along the rooftops. He's not liking the lack of control. *Paedors are used to the firm ground.*

"It's okay, Dunn. They're just helping us past the minefield."

"I hope so. We've been delayed enough."

52

Dunn

The minefield. I don't know anything about it or why someone would bury explosive weapons in the dirt, but at a distance it looks harmless. The stretch of roots, dark soil, and spots of grass is our direct path to Brigandre.

"I'm climbing down first," I say.

I've got Katlene strapped to my back again after a few hours of letting Riverduna carry her. I'm cautious as I make my way down from Nameus and I feel immediate relief when my boots are flat on dirt instead of slate.

"Listen carefully," Autana says when she touches the ground. "We must walk in two separate groups. Riverduna follows right behind me. And you, Dunn, follow right behind Skyntar. Do not divert for any reason or we will all be blown up."

The reality hits me only after I look down and see human remains… bone and skull fragments, woven through the field's core. And then I see intact corpses. Trails of dried blood. Bits of clothing from Paedors and Skies alike.

"Why did they come here?" Riverduna asks.

I know that she's referring to the corpses.

"Fools. Assassins. All of them sent out on a blind death march."

"How long has this field existed?"

"Near as long as the districts." Autana talks as she walks backward, her wiry body prancing over gnarled roots. "But we don't know when the death traps were put here."

I'm not dying out here. I'm not about to be blown up while staring at my dream.

Brigandre. Less than a mile away. I don't know what I'll find inside the tower, but I'm hoping it's not what Mama told me. I'm hoping for a miracle.

53

Riverduna

We move cautiously through the minefield, until I'm forced to stop fast when Autana swings her arm back and tosses something to me. A metal whistle. A different shape than the wooden one Dunn gave me.

"I already have a whistle, Autana."

"This is in case you need help from Skies. And only Skies." She looks over to where Dunn and Skyntar are walking. "Should your Paedor friend betray you."

"He wouldn't hurt me."

"Brigandre is a trap. You should be aware of that fact, Riverduna. Whether or not you trust Dunn… it won't matter once you walk into that tower."

"We'll be fine," I say. "But I'll keep your whistle too." I hang it around my neck next to the wooden whistle. *I won't need either of them.*

* * *

"This is it," Skyntar says. He's the first to step off the field and onto the stone that surrounds the entrance. "Brigandre."

I breathe lightly as I follow them, watching the expression on Dunn's face when he tilts his head back to gaze up at the tower.

"So many windows," I say.

"Yeah."

"We'll leave you to it," Autana says. She trades looks with her brother and they circle away from me and Dunn. "Riverduna, don't hesitate to call for help. Trust the high ground."

"I will," I say.

As quickly as they had appeared in the attic, Autana and Skyntar vanish in the fog. I can hear their footsteps as they run back the way we came.

54

Dunn

"We'll work faster if we split up," River says. "I'll take the even floors, you take the odds."

Her confidence astounds me. "Take it easy, darlie. We don't know if the floors and stairs are secure."

"But I want to help you. What are we looking for anyway?"

I keep my voice at a whisper as I pass through the doorway. I hear Katlene babbling against my back. "Ravabrig symbols and writing."

"But you can't read, right?"

"Right. I'll call you to come read it if I find something."

Riverduna pushes past me, bouncing in place as she surveys the large floor. "Can I look for photographs?"

"I doubt that you will find anything of use or pleasure here, darlie."

"But can I look?"

"Go ahead. I'll keep Katlene with me."

Riverduna hums the Echo Song as she goes up a stairway to our right. I decide against telling her to be quiet. The way this tower looks… no one has lived here for a hundred years.

Chaos catalyst.

I go from room to room on the first floor, finding nothing but broken glass.

Anarchy. Darkness.

The third floor has a long, white corridor. What I see on the floors and walls makes me vomit.

Needles. Saws. Streaks of blood. And body parts. Skulls. No more than a few days could have passed since these kills were made. *Brigandre isn't abandoned.*

"River!" I yell out.

She doesn't call back to me.

"River!"

Shit. Katlene starts to cry and I take her off my back, instead holding her in my arms. "River, where are you?"

I charge up the stairs, up to the fourth, fifth, sixth floors, then halt at the seventh floor. *Hell no.* A door is flung wide open to the first room in the corridor, and there are bodies of children on the floor. All dead. *And all girls.*

"Dunn?"

No. I back out of the room, looking for Riverduna. "Darlie, no. Stay where you are. Wait for me."

"I'll just go back down," she says. Her voice is echoing from above. She sounds excited. "I found some pressed flowers in books!"

There isn't a solution to the anarchy. I back out of the corpse-filled room and head back to the first floor. *It's a death sentence.*

"Riverduna," I call. I exhale when we see each other again at the bottom. "Did you find any writings or symbols?"

"No. Well, there were some numbers written on the walls. But I didn't see anything relating to the Ravabrigs."

"I think this is bigger than any one of the gangs," I say. "But I was wrong to bring you with me. I should've left you and Katlene with Harvest or even Anglaus."

Riverduna tilts her head, looking confused. "We're still alive, aren't we?"

"I don't need to keep looking for evidence," I say. "It's all around us."

She turns and points to the back wall. "Did you look at that?"

I follow her eyes and see small squiggles of red in the bottom corner. "Writing." *So there is a message here.*

Riverduna holds onto the book that she found and bends down to read the words on the wall for me. "'They will not know it's been taken from them. The ground and the sky. Or it will belong to no one. Send them to the shadows. Ready the fires. Sacrifice. December 2098, my brethren. We will have control.'"

Every word I hear weakens my legs until they give out. I fall on my knees in front of the wall. *They're targeting both worlds. The children.*

Riverduna keeps reading, not seeming to comprehend the meaning of it. *How is she not seeing what I'm seeing?*

"'Sacrificium feminae.'"

Sacrifice women...

"'Exscindo arbiter.'"

Witness to annihilation...

"'Deceptio vinculum.'"

Deceive to enslave...

"And all these names in the last line," she says, running her finger along the wall. "Current's name, and Amos… and so many others. All men."

I stare blankly. My head is spinning. My legs are numb. "The gangs, darlie. All of them signed it."

She still doesn't react. Doesn't panic.

What the bloody hell have I done?

Somehow Riverduna is lost in her own world. She looks down at the book in her hands, flipping through it with the eyes of a child. It's like she can block out the darkness. She's somehow impervious to evil.

"Dunn, look at this one. It's a pressed hyacinth. And this, an edelweiss!"

Riverduna. Beautiful Riverduna. Tears fill my eyes as I listen to her gush about flowers. Such a small thing cheers her heart. She doesn't realize... She doesn't see the dead end.

55

Riverduna

I read a page of the book, realizing it's all about the flowers that are pressed into it. It seems out of place for such a beautiful book to be in this dilapidated tower. *Reminds me of the attic.*

"Darlie," Dunn says.

I turn to the next page and look up. "What?"

He puts Katlene on the floor, wrapping a blanket around her, and comes close, gently taking the book from me.

"Darlie," he says again.

I see him struggle to speak. "I want to kiss you."

"Kiss me?"

"I wish you to know how I feel." He holds my hands in his, drawing me against him. "How I feel about us."

Dunn... Dunn wants to kiss me.

I can feel him shaking as he says, "May I kiss you, Riverduna?"

I look into his face, my heart pounding. *He has protected me. Loved me.* He has become my world.

"As a gentleman would do," I whisper.

Dunn leans forward, staring long into my eyes, then lightly presses his lips to my cheek.

Not like Current.

Then Dunn kisses me softly on the lips, circling his arms around my waist. A tingly warmth rushes through me.

I breathe out hard.

"Are you okay?" he asks.

I nod. But I can't lie. "I'm scared."

"Me too," he says. "I'm terrified."

56

Dunn

"You have to run," I whisper.

"What?"

"Run to Nameus." *The Ravabrigs are coming.*

Riverduna steps back. The softness in her face changes to fear.

"I'll come find you," I say. "Run."

"What do you mean?" She keeps her eyes on me as I lift Katlene into my arms. "Dunn…"

"Run, Riverduna. You have to run. Here. Take Katy with you."

She's confused by my frantic voice but takes Katlene. "I don't want to go back without you."

"You have to. You have to go." I gesture to the hall separating us from the entrance. "Now, River!"

Just as she hesitantly turns to leave, all sixteen of the Ravabrigs walk into the room.

"Did you find what you were looking for, Dunn?" Current asks.

Riverduna is frozen. Her shallow, rapid breaths are the only thing I hear.

"So? The catalyst? Anarchy?" Current walks over to me while the others form a circle around Riverduna and Katlene. "Tell me, Dunn.

What have you learned?"

I can barely steady myself as I look past him. Hywill is carrying the branding iron like it's a trophy. Not one of them is speaking. They're just staring Riverduna down, savoring the hunt. They are each armed with a shotgun and pistol.

"Don't hurt her," I say. "Please, Current."

"That's a stupid thing to say." Current takes Katlene from Riverduna's arms. He walks her around the room with a calculated pace, worrying me that any second he will drop her. "I would never hurt my beloved Riverduna. Neither would I hurt this little girl."

"Give Katy to me."

"Of course." He places her in my arms as if he planned to do so all along. "I've no use for her yet."

"Brotherhood," I say. "All the gangs are working together, aren't they?"

Current says nothing. He makes one small motion with his hand and three of the Ravabrigs violently force Riverduna to the floor.

"Help me out now, Dunn. We do this together."

Riverduna is trying to fight back. Her angry screams dissolve into sobs when Current kneels down to speak to her.

I'm not a Ravabrig.

"Make her one of us. Get this over with," Raelot says to me.

I look from him to Hywill, who's bringing the iron over.

Sacrificium feminae. I shut my eyes thinking of those words. *Demons. I've been a friend to the dark.*

"Dunn, make the Sky mine."

Sky. I let out a wheezing breath. *Riverduna is more than just a Sky.*

"Take my winnings, Current."

"What?"

"I'll serve your family. Own me."

Own me instead of her.

I love her.

"I'll give everything to you," I say. "Everything. My house, my weapons, every fight that is left in me. Even if I have to kill a thousand people in the pit, Current, I'll do it. In whatever way you wish to see it done."

Current looks at me and looks back at Riverduna. "Suppose that's a trick of yours," he says. "I let River go and you end up lying to me."

"No. I'll let you do it now. Make me the victim now. Beat me, Current. Go on."

Current stands and tells the boys to release Riverduna. He shakes his head while looking me up and down. "How much of a fool are you?"

"Give Katlene to River," I say. "Let them go free."

"And then?"

I swallow hard before answering. I look into his glowering eyes. "Hit me. I won't fight back."

Current gives a subtle nod and takes Katlene from me to give to Riverduna. Within ten seconds of feeling relief for the girls, I'm pistol-whipped in the face.

"Dunn!"

I try to tell her to run, knowing that Current could change his mind at any moment, but I'm struck again.

"Take care of him, Wheelden," Current says.

I'm dragged along the floor and thrown against the wall, before I manage to let out a hoarse scream. "Go, Riverduna! Run!"

Current paces next to my head, swinging his shotgun like the edge of a sword. "You know I love a good chase, right? A broken deal equals a just punishment."

No... I try to roll over, but Wheelden stomps on my chest. A sharp pain spreads through my ribs.

"Although I really hope it doesn't take too long to catch my little sparrow." Current looks down at me with a devil's gleam in his eyes.

"Otherwise she'll end up like the corpses in this place."

River...

"Raelot! Enbraet! Bring her to the Brigehouse!"

Run.

"This is the game you want to play, Duncan?"

I see the shadow of Current's gun right before I black out.

57

Riverduna

I run away from Brigandre and toward the minefield, blowing the whistle that the Sky twins gave me. I'm struggling to move any faster with Katlene in my arms.

"Riverduna! Come on!"

Autana.

I run after her and glance over my shoulder to see Skyntar not far behind.

"Stay close to me," Autana says. "We'll make it back to Nameus."

"Faster!" Skyntar yells. "They sent Ravabrigs after us!"

They have guns. They'll shoot.

"Switch paths, Skyntar!" Autana says to her brother.

I'm baffled as I watch them change course, jumping diagonally from one patch of dirt to another.

"Follow me, River," Skyntar says, waving an arm over his head.

I remain as close as I can to him, breathing in the cold air. *The fog is coming in. Perfect cover.*

* * *

"It was a massacre in the tower, right? Bodies everywhere."

"What?"

Skyntar wastes no time in questioning me about Brigandre. Once we're back in Nameus, his chattering is relentless.

"I didn't see bodies in there," I say.

"No? Then you were either temporarily blind or daydreaming, Riverduna. The Paedors put gory messages on every wall and crevice."

"They aren't all bad people. And I found colorful books. Maybe there would be some photographs in there too, but I didn't have time to look."

"You're not using your head, girl. There is nothing but corruption in Dredgar. I knew we couldn't trust a Paedor."

Dunn saved me. I would've been trapped with Current for the rest of my life. "He was trying to help, Skyntar. He's trying to protect the children in the streets. But he wants peace for the Skies too."

Skyntar walks forward, cornering me against a chimney. "Dunn led you into that trap."

"He wouldn't hurt me," I say. I kiss Katlene's head and bounce with her when she starts crying.

"Well, have you seen him kill someone?"

I look away, instantly picturing Dunn covered in blood.

"Yeah?" Skyntar spreads his arms, raising his voice as he continues to rant. "What was that like? Was he a good Paedor then?"

"Why are you so angry at Dunn?" I ask. "He didn't do anything to you."

Skyntar huffs and turns away, snapping his fingers in a gesture that leads Autana to step in and talk to me.

"Some Skies could care less about the existence of Dredgar, River, but one year ago, two Paedor men murdered our mother. She was minding her own business, whistling along with the sparrows on her walk to the river. Then a hail of bullets struck. Her face and skull were mutilated."

I watch her look down and sniff hard before returning her eyes to me.

"I know you think you can trust your friend. But you're still a Sky, Riverduna. And even if you prefer solitude, you should have a strong group of friends around you."

I shrug, not knowing what to say. Of the few other Skies I've met outside of my family, I know no others on the rooftops.

"We can change that," Autana says with a smile. "Come on. Meet some new friends."

58

Dunn

"C'mon, Dunn. Wake up. We got a lot to talk about."

I blink hard and lift my head, groaning at the throbbing pain. Current is pacing the Brigehouse, whiskey in hand. Bramy stands at the door with a rifle, avoiding looking in my direction, but I know he's paying attention to everything that Current is saying.

I'm chained to a chair. *Surprised I'm not maimed yet. And I still have my other eye.*

"Here's the thing, Dunn," Current says. He looks thrilled to see that I'm conscious again. "I want to start this off as a gentleman." He sits in the chair across from me, crossing one knee over the other like he's about to tell me a long story. "Anything that you tell me is pointless in saving the Skies. They and their homes will be blown up at dawn."

Dawn. It's still night?

"Well, not dawn exactly. I plan to set the explosives off before the sun rises."

"Destroying Nameus means destroying every house and family in Dredgar too. Why bother setting us all on fire?" I say.

"Chaos is the catalyst for change. Isn't that what we all want, Dunn? A little change in society? A new order?"

I scowl at his wicked smile. "The Ravabrigs have done more than enough. You can't have Riverduna."

"No?" Current leans forward, spitting in my eye when he says, "Tell me where she is."

"The writing on the wall. Was that you or Amos?"

"I'd like her to be alive, Dunn. I'd like to marry my little sparrow."

"You know I'd die with them," I say. "I'd proudly die with the Skies."

"Which attic is she in?"

"No."

I brace myself in the chair as I watch Current lose patience. He stands and goes into the back room, returning moments later holding a serrated knife. "You saw more of Nameus than any of us."

"Your boys can find her without me, Current."

"Look. You see this blade? I'm cutting you, Dunn. I'm gonna make sure you can't grip a sword or gun ever again."

"I used to trust your family," I say. "We used to play pretend soldiers as children. Then you switched from a toy knife to a real one." I raise my voice as Current presses the tip of the knife against my fingers. "I was ten when you did that to me. Ten!"

Current grabs my wrist with his other hand and slashes the knife. I hear myself cry out and look at the floor. Two fingers gone. Blood streaming.

Current angrily screams in my face. "I am the one who lights the fuse! I will set the explosions off. No matter what you say! I could slit your throat or remove your head, Dunn. But torture is adequate for a disobedient Ravabrig like you."

I force myself to slow my breathing. I close my remaining three fingers into a fist. The rush of pain will come after the shock subsides. *But I still have an intact left hand.*

"You can't do any worse to me than what Amos did," I say.

Current pours himself more whiskey. He's acting so calm, like he just did me a favor. "Shut up about my father."

"You hurt Riverduna and Amos hurt me."

"I should just knock you out again and be done with it."

"But you want to find her before you blow it all up. Right?"

He glowers at me until Bramy approaches. "Hey Cure, you better go outside."

"Why?"

"Coald has one of your pistols."

"It's the middle of the night. Let him play with it."

"Well, he's not playing," Bramy says. He gives me a mischievous look. "He's taking it apart."

Current slams his whiskey down. "What?"

"Yeah. It's one of your old ones. The vintage sort that you had in a case."

"Bloody hell." Current heads for the door, pointing back at me. "Watch him, Bramy. I'll be back."

As soon as Current is gone, Bramy starts taking the chains off of me. I'm still finding myself looking down at my severed fingers. I don't know why I'm getting his help. *Maybe he was reminded of his brother...*

"Why the compassion?" I ask. "Did this bring back memories of Esann? Or are you just—"

"Shh. We have to get out now. C'mon!" Bramy pulls me up and pushes me toward the door. "Go, go! To the left, Dunn."

"Why are you doing this?"

"Look, I've wanted revenge for what they did to my brother ever since that day. But that's not why I set up Coald's little stunt to distract Current."

I can't help smiling. *Bringing little Coald into the act. Good call.*

"It's Amos," Bramy says.

"What?"

"I went through the same thing that you did. He did it to me too. If we don't warn the Skies, they will all become slaves to Current's family. And the children of the streets will be tied to Amos. I'm not letting that happen."

I run after him as he goes further down the alley. "Where are we going?"

"Anglaus. They can help us fight back."

"No, they won't."

"Trust me," he says.

"I don't. I don't trust them either. Why in the world would Anglaus help us defend the Skies?"

Bramy stops and turns around. "Because Sashae owes me for protecting her daughter."

"When was this, Bramy?"

"Three years ago."

Wow. Lies, disloyalty, and mutiny against the Ravabrigs. All in the same night.

Bramy makes a comment on the state of my hand and we stand in the middle of the alley while he quickly wraps it up.

Bold of you, Bramy. Bloody bold of you to take my side.

* * *

It takes less than two minutes for us to convince Sashae to let us into the Anglaus house, and I'm happy and relieved to see Tempest alive and well among the feisty group of women. She drinks a bottle of red wine while listening to me and Bramy, and most of the others are sitting at one long table with piles of cards and bottles of rum. We had apparently interrupted their drinking game night.

"We haven't much time before the attack," I say. "Can you spare weapons and clothes for the Skies?"

"They don't know anything about fighting."

"Just help them blend in. I'm doing this for all of us, Sashae."

"And what's it to you besides saving Riverduna and your sister?"

"The children. The Ravabrigs are going to bring Nameus down, and in that destruction, they will turn every innocent person into a slave. Dredgar will be worse than it ever has."

Sashae sits in a rocking chair, looking like a very traditional Paedor woman with her hair in a circle braid and a long, wide skirt and boots. She's started on her second cigarette.

"I admit I'm not fond of Anglaus," I say. "Various reasons for it. But I want to see you remain free too. Women of all ages should stand against Current."

She takes a drag from her cigarette. "And what will you and Bramy be doing while we defend your asses?"

Bramy answers for me. "We're gonna shoot the cables to bring down our water supply."

I look at him when he says this, realizing I need to go along with the idea. But I don't know how he thought that up so fast.

"All of it?" Sashae asks.

"It's the only water we've got to suppress the fire. And there will be fire."

Sashae looks at me with a slight smile as she understands my thoughts on the matter.

"Clearly you're making this up as you go," she says.

"We don't know when Ferrelium and the Culmordis will run out," I say. "We have to be ready for an attack by all of them."

"The gangs are united, Sashae," Bramy tells her. "Working together. They have more power."

"No." She suddenly stands up, throwing her cigarette to the floor. "Like hell they are."

I notice all the women rise from the table in one rehearsed motion, and they all go to pick up their guns.

"Lead the way, boys," Tempest says with her usual fiery grin. She winks at me as she lifts her shotgun. "Let's rain bullets."

59

Riverduna

"He's dead, River. And if not yet, he will be soon."

I look at the faces of the other Skies gathered around us. Dozens of them are scattered across a cluster of rooftops, all paying close attention to what Autana and Skyntar are saying about Dunn and the Ravabrigs.

"He'll make it," I say. "He will."

"You stay up here with the baby, and we'll help raise her. The danger isn't in Nameus."

"What if the gangs come to kill more of us? We need to be ready to fight them."

"No, girl," a grey-haired Sky says. "You know Skies don't fight. We don't fight anyone."

"But what if they come?"

"We hide."

I suppress a whimper, frustrated to be standing alone among my own people.

"We can do more than just hide," I say.

"Come on." Autana waves me over as several Skies head into the nearest attic. "We can talk later."

I shake my head at her, backing away with Katlene. *Dunn's coming.* I decide to go to a different spot on the rooftops to be alone.

"Your brother's alive, Katy," I whisper. "He is." I touch a hand to my neck, feeling the sharp cold of the metal whistle. *The Sky whistle. But where's the one from Dunn?* I look down. The other cord is gone.

I lost the wooden whistle.

"No…" I sit down on the slate. *How's he gonna find me? Miles and miles of rooftops in fog. Where will he come from?*

"Shh," I say as Katlene cries. "Shh, baby girl." I try bouncing while sitting, and she only fusses louder, her little body wriggling in my arms. "Katy, it's okay." I stand back up, walking from one side of the roof to the other. I begin humming the Echo Song, hoping to calm her down.

Dunn, where are you?

"Aquila volans, libertas, libertas." I sing out loud. "Aquila volans, auferet—"

Then I hear another voice singing with me.

"—Nox libertas, libertas. Aquila volans."

I turn around. *It's Dunn.*

"Dunn!"

"River." He smiles as I run into his arms.

"I knew you'd come back."

"Yeah." He gives Katlene a kiss on the cheek and cups my face in his hands, kissing my lips. "We have to speak with the Skies."

I hear the tension in his voice and look at the bandages on his hand. "Did Current do that to you?"

"Don't worry about it. You met up with Autana and Skyntar again, right?"

"Yes, but…" I stare past him, seeing Bramy come through the fog, along with Sashae from Anglaus. "What are they doing here?"

"Bramy's with us, darlie. So is Anglaus."

I gently touch his bandaged hand, cringing when I see the blood from his wounds. "Dunn, the Skies still don't trust you." I can see the worry in his face. "They won't trust any Paedors."

"The Skies will be killed off if we don't help. You have to make them listen."

"I don't know if I can."

60

Dunn

I'm facing a circle of suspicious Skies, each of them staring at me like I'm pointing a loaded gun at their heads. "You either trust me or you don't. But the Ravabrigs are going to destroy Nameus. There are explosives planted in every attic."

"What can we do to stop the attack?" Autana asks.

"There is no stopping it. We have to fight back."

"Revenge does nothing for us," Skyntar says. He looks around, waiting for nods of agreement from other Skies. For some reason he and his sister are speaking for everyone else.

Bramy comes forward, stopping inches from Skyntar's face. "Think you are free now, Sky? You won't stay free without a fight. A bloody, dirty, bastard of a fight." He brings his fist up beside his head and gives a sharp grunt. "You all make them pay."

"Bramy," I say, "your speech isn't working."

He trades an irritated look with me and steps back.

"You will all be slaves of the Ravabrigs," Sashae calls out. Her booming voice snaps in the night. "If you don't stand against them. We must face them together."

"And why would we work with you?" A redheaded Sky yells back.

"The enemy of the Skies is the enemy of us all," Sashae says. "We bear the same scars. The same losses."

Riverduna comes between the group of Skies and Sashae. She hands Katlene over to Tempest before speaking up. "What's the plan, Dunn?"

"You have to dress as Paedors," I say. "Each of you will choose to either stay here with a weapon or join us on the streets. I advise for most of you to come down to Dredgar. The explosions will blow apart the rooftops and we don't know where and how many there will be. But you can blend in on the ground and hide. The women of Anglaus will lead you to the safest places."

I look at Sashae, who nods approvingly.

"We must go now," she says. "Make a choice. Stay here or go to the streets."

I watch the Skies talk amongst themselves, and one by one, they begin following Anglaus off the rooftops.

"I'll take Katlene with me," Tempest says. "She'll be safe the whole time."

"Thank you," I say. "You ready, Bramy?"

But Bramy is already halfway down to the streets.

61

Riverduna

"You coming, darlie?"

"I'm staying here."

"No." Dunn steps away from the edge, coming back to me. "The fires will be everywhere."

"I'm staying," I say. "I won't risk Current taking me again. I'll be okay, Dunn."

He exhales loudly and looks off to the side, seeing Skyntar watching us.

"Okay." Dunn lowers his voice, pulling me into an embrace. "When the explosions start, you run. Just run."

I nod.

"Run," he says again as he backs toward the edge.

"I will."

He hesitates in his descent, but eventually disappears to the ground, enveloped in the fog. I cross my arms where he held me, still feeling his warmth. *Be careful, Dunn.*

"Hey, River."

I look at Skyntar as he approaches me. He's holding something in his fist.

"You dropped this on our way back to Nameus."

I gasp when he opens his hand. *The wooden whistle.* He waits for me to take it and steps back when I clutch it tightly to my chest.

"I never wanted to trust Dunn, but I see that I was wrong." He moves toward the edge of the rooftops, looking back as he says, "Dunn loves you. Proof enough. Good luck, Riverduna."

"Good luck, Skyntar," I say.

62

Dunn

"Bramy, you know my aim is nothing like yours."

"I know."

I glance up to where the cables should be. I can't see them in the dark.

"I don't have a trigger finger either anymore," I say.

"Well, you do what you can. I'll be across the street."

"No light. It's gonna be a tricky shot."

Bramy grins. "I'm just gonna shoot, Dunn. I'll hit something."

Dammit. This is going to be bad.

I duck down in the alley and watch him walk across to the other side. He points his rifle to the sky and waits.

Where's Current?

I know he won't be far behind us. Every noise makes my heart pound, and I barely breathe. We are just waiting.

A gunshot cracks the silence, and I look to where Bramy is positioned. He's crouching with his rifle aimed up.

I try to get a good grip on my rifle, brushing the trigger with my left hand. But I'm shaking. I can't hold it right.

Another gunshot.

I glance in Bramy's direction again.

He's down.

He's not moving.

"Bramy," I start to call out.

An explosion rocks the ground.

Vicious shouts echo from all sides. *Ravabrigs. Ferrelium. Culmordis.*

63

Riverduna

Nameus is on fire. I hear the screams of Skies around me. I run, leaping over a huge gap in the rooftops, crying out when I slip upon landing. My clothes are burning. Smoke stings my eyes. *Get off the roof.*

I make my way toward the edge, but lose my breath when I see the mass of violence beneath me. The gangs are killing Skies. Swords, guns, knives.

"River! Riverduna!"

I crawl back the way I came, the smoke and flames cutting off my path downward.

"Riverduna! I'm here!"

Sashae has come back to the roof. She's motioning for me to follow her. "Come on, girl!"

I reach out to her, feeling tears forming in my eyes. "I need a weapon," I say. "I need a weapon down there."

"I know. I'll keep you safe."

I don't feel anything but terror when I reach the ground again. Sashae keeps looking at me to make sure I'm still with her as we run.

I need a gun. *Dunn's shotgun blade.*

64

Dunn

I try again to aim for the cables overhead. *The water.* Everything is burning. My fingers won't grip the rifle. Even when I try to prop it in a different way, my breathing is so rapid that I can't aim straight.

Blood is flying in the streets. The Sky twins are firing pistols, flanked by Anglaus.

Smoke stings my eyes as I step out from the alley. The fires are spreading.

"Hell," I whisper, lifting my rifle in the middle of the cobblestone. *C'mon, Dunn. You can do this.*

A heavy force knocks me down. Raelot. He runs past me, fixated on another victim.

"Hey, Dunn."

I get up, chest tightening when I see who's behind me.

Current.

I swing my rifle against his sword. He snarls, pushing me back.

"You're only good at grappling and biting, aren't you?"

My knees buckle. I grit my teeth as I try to fight him.

"I'm not letting you out of this."

My arms are trembling. He's going to take my head off either way.

"Cheater," I snarl. "You always have to have the upper hand."

"Cheat? You think this is a fight between little boys, Dunn? This is Ravabrig will."

I grunt as he pushes me to my knees. *I'm not dying like this. I can't.*

A thunder of gunfire turns Current's attention and Bramy charges, knocking into his ass like an avenging boar.

Bramy. He's still alive.

I scramble backward, breathing heavily as I watch the two duel. Bramy's taking hits from Current but coming back with equally strong swings. *He's doing this for Esann. I know this. And he's doing it for all the other boys... the ones who never saw justice.*

65

Riverduna

"Dunn's house," I say. "I need to get to his house."

"This way," Sashae replies.

We run through alleys lined with fire, ducking into the shadows when we see the gangs.

"Back. Back!"

I follow her around a corner, unable to recognize anything. Bits of brick and rubble are scattered across the cobblestone.

"Here! In here!"

Sashae pulls open the door and pushes me ahead of her.

Shotgun blade. I sprint through the house, looking for the gun.

I'm going to fight.

66

Dunn

Current backs away from Bramy, looking like he's ready to give up.

But I know better. It's not over.

This is an execution.

Two Ferreliums run out from the alley, swords raised. Bramy screams at them as he fires his gun. One falls. But the other looks at Current as Current picks up the dead Ferrelium's sword.

Bramy's finger is on the trigger as three swords pierce his body. His eyes are still on Current when he slumps to the ground, and he turns his head in my direction when the final cut is made across his throat.

Dammit.

A sob escapes me as the Ferrelium walks away.

Bramy. Dammit.

Tears and smoke blind me as I fumble with my rifle. I can feel Current circling me.

"All right, Dunn, so you tried to save the day. Let me end your humiliation. I'll cut off both your arms and take your other eye. Then you can tell me I've found your weakness."

Bloody hell.

Riverduna.

I stop fumbling with the rifle when I see her standing behind Current.

"Losing an appendage is not my weakness," I say. I look past Current, gazing at Riverduna's fighter stance as she wields my shotgun blade. "She is."

One shot echoes.

Then another.

Current never turns.

He stares at me, blood spurting from his neck, down his chest. Riverduna screams wildly and sprints forward, ramming the blade through his body. Anger in her raspy voice, pain streaming with her tears.

The other gang members are giving us threatening looks as they back away from the scene of death. The attack has ceased. A wordless truce among us. *But they will retaliate. One day they will.*

Current falls. He's breathed his last.

I stand, unable to speak, unable to move.

"Survivors." Tempest's soft voice breaks through the silence.

I look back at her as she touches a fist to her chest and holds it up in a sign of pride.

Survivors. We are.

* * *

Sashae comes forward and holds out her hand. She smiles when I grasp it, and gives a nod to Riverduna.

"Thank you," I say.

Show 'em Anglaus justice, Sashae.

"What do we do now?" Riverduna asks.

I gaze up at the smoldering rooftops and around at the blood-soaked cobblestone streets. Tempest hands off a babbling Katlene to Riverduna, who's waiting with outstretched arms.

"Let's go," I say.

"Where?"

"Somewhere safe." I smile into Riverduna's eyes. "Somewhere just for us, darlie."

Sashae cordially sends us off, hollering out an order for members of Anglaus to defend us as we go.

We run north.

And we don't look back.

67

Riverduna

Dunn and I have a new home. The belfry of Brigandre. Only I think we're going to change the name of the tower. Something to match our family life… and maybe to honor our son Bramley.

There is still a lawless society out there. Still a place of violence, anger, and toil. The fragmented Ravabrigs and the other gangs routinely spar with Anglaus. And many Skies now unleash devious pranks on the Paedors. It's certainly a mess, and Dunn and I have a lot of work to do here. But if a Paedor can love a Sky, I'd say we can all learn to live in peace.

Trust the high ground. That's how we win.

About the Author

Han M Greenbarg has been in love with writing fiction since childhood. She is an avid coffee drinker, proud dog mom, and lover of country music and war movies. Her biggest jolts of inspiration stem from nature, a variety of film scores, and animals of all kind.

You can connect with me on:
- https://www.hanmgreenbarg.com
- https://www.instagram.com/hanmgreenbargauthor

Also by Han M Greenbarg

Scurts Flightplan

With three months left to live in a stifling, post-nuclear city, Damon Scurto believes he has one last shot at finding the grave of the woman who got away. He is best friends with a guy who eats paper, best frenemies with a convicted killer, and is the bane of his wine-drunk therapist's existence.

Elf Bat Book One Kiah

Twelve years after the ruthless massacre of his parents and most of his kin, eighteen-year-old Elf Bat Kiah lives a life of internalized grief and solitude in his family's cave. The arrival of Fly, a reckless purebred Elf maiden, sparks the flame for revenge and a resurgence of the Bats.

Elf Bat Book Two Sacrifice

The revenge of the Elf Bats has begun in Sidhovvn, each Bat warrior facing down the count who carried out the ruthless slaughter of their family. But in the midst of seeking justice against the purebred king and his soldiers, the sudden emergence of Fly's demon-driven adoptive mother Ixetmori proves to be the bigger test of wills, and the defining moment of what it means to be courageous.

Chehnuh

Year 2018. Chehnuh, a half-elven and sole survivor of his people's genocide, resides quietly in a remote cabin in the Sierra Nevada mountains. No one knows how he came to the United States. No one knows that he is part Elf. He is a mystery to all who meet him until a young widowed mother interrupts his peaceful life with a baby and the shadow of a deadly stalker, forever changing how Chehnuh sees his own past, humanity, and the heroic role he has yet to play in today's world.

Byrne

Imagination is survival. That's what he tells them. Full of weird quirks and crazy story ideas, novelist Maddox Byrne can't figure out how to connect with normal people. Ever since the lockdown began and the residents of Tower 881 were trapped together, all he's wanted was to keep morale high and finally get the woman of his dreams to notice him. But every person has a breaking point. Every person longs for what they can't have. How long can humanity live in distrust and paranoia? How long before every person loses their mind? Imagination. Imagination is survival. But can it really save us?

Firemartenn

Blamed for his father's death and the doom of Ateinekus, fifteen-year-old Jet must prove his worth as Firemartenn to the village elders. But the fire dragon king won't let just anyone reach the sacred Ackellhnn's sapphire. Jet has to play by Feuskarg's rules in order to save his family and be the hero he's always wanted to be.